NATIONAL BESTSELLER

Longlisted for the Scotiabank Giller Prize

Praise for Annabel Lyon and

### THE SWEET GIRL

"Lyon [has] established herself as this generation's answer to Alice Munro. A master of wordplay and storytelling, Lyon takes readers deep into the hearts and secret desires of her characters."
*The Vancouver Sun*

"A remarkable novel, not just a pleasure to read but also a book that I expect to reread several times." Jeet Heer, *National Post*

"Annabel Lyon is a sharp, funny, and subversive writer. . . . What is exhilarating about Lyon's work is that she has enough confidence in her imagination and her craft so that she can borrow from the best and still create art that is absolutely her own."
*Quill & Quire*

"I can't think of a writer with a better command of the English language." *Ottawa Citizen*

"Lyon is no mouse, and her roar will not soon subside."
*The Globe and Mail*

"Lyon has done the requisite homework . . . and convincingly mixes the modern with the ancient." *Toronto Star*

Annabel Lyon

# THE
# SWEET
# GIRL

A NOVEL

VINTAGE CANADA

VINTAGE CANADA EDITION, 2013

Published in Canada by Vintage Canada, a division of Random House of Canada
Limited, Toronto, in 2013. Originally published in hardcover in Canada by
Random House Canada, a division of Random House of Canada Limited, in 2012.
Distributed by Random House of Canada Limited.

Vintage Canada with colophon is a registered trademark.

This book is a work of fiction. Names, characters, places and incidents either are the
product of the author's imagination or are used fictitiously. Any resemblance to
actual persons, living or dead, events or locales is entirely coincidental.

www.randomhouse.ca

Library and Archives Canada Cataloguing in Publication

Lyon, Annabel, 1971–
The sweet girl / Annabel Lyon.

ISBN 978-0-307-35945-2

1. Aristotle—Fiction. 2. Greece—History—Macedonian Expansion, 359–323 B.C.—Fiction.
I. Title.

PS8573.Y62S94 2013      C813'.6      C2012-902048-6

Text and cover design by Terri Nimmo

Image credits: Daniel Murtagh/Trevillion Images

Printed and bound in the United States of America

2 4 6 8 9 7 5 3 1

*for Bryant,*
*guardian of my solitude*

AND WHEN THE GIRL SHALL BE GROWN UP she shall be given in marriage to Nicanor; but if anything happen to the girl (which heaven forbid and no such thing will happen) before her marriage, or when she is married but before there are children, Nicanor shall have full powers, both with regard to the child and with regard to everything else, to administer in a manner worthy both of himself and of us.                    *Aristotle's will*

CAST OF CHARACTERS

ARISTOTLE'S HOUSEHOLD

Pythias, known as Pytho: *Aristotle's daughter by his dead wife,*
   *also named Pythias*
Aristotle: *a philosopher*
Herpyllis: *Aristotle's concubine, formerly a servant*
Nicomachus, known as Nico: *Aristotle's son by Herpyllis*
Tycho: *a slave of Aristotle*
Jason, known as Myrmex: *a poor relation and adopted son of Aristotle*
Pyrrhaios: *a slave of Aristotle*
Simon: *a free servant of Aristotle*
Thale: *a free servant of Aristotle*
Ambracis: *a slave of Aristotle*
Olympios: *a slave of Aristotle*
Pretty: *Olympios's daughter, a slave of Aristotle*
Philo: *a slave of Aristotle*

Akakios: *a rival to Aristotle and guest at Aristotle's symposia*
Krios: *a city administrator and guest at Aristotle's symposia*
Gaiane: *a friend of Pythias*
Theophrastos: *Aristotle's successor as head of the Lyceum*

Thaulos: *leader of the Macedonian garrison*
Plios: *a magistrate*
Glycera: *a widow*
Euphranor: *a cavalry officer*
Demetrios: *a slave of Euphranor*
A priestess of Artemis
Meda, Obole, Aphrodisia: *"daughters" of Glycera*
Clea: *a midwife*
Candaules: *a dog-breeder, Clea's companion*
Dionysus: *a god*
Nicanor: *Pythias's cousin*

# CONTENTS

I. . . . . . . . . . . . . . . . . . . . .1

II. . . . . . . . . . . . . . . . . .119

III . . . . . . . . . . . . . . . . .207

I

The first time I ask to carry a knife to the temple, Daddy tells me I'm not allowed to because we're Macedonian. Here in Athens, you have to be born an Athenian girl to carry the basket with the knife, to lead the procession to the sacrifice. The Athenians can be awfully snotty, even all these years after our army defeated their army.

"I want to see, though," I say. I have seven summers. "If you carry the basket, you get to watch from right up front."

"I know, pet."

The next morning he takes me to the market. Crowds part for him respectfully; Macedonian or not, he's famous, my daddy. "Which one?" he asks.

I take my time choosing. It's late spring, baby season, and there are calves and piglets and trays of pullets too. Around us, men speak of the army and when it will return; surely soon, now that the Persians are defeated and their king is on the run. I finally choose a white lamb crying for its mother and we walk it home. I hold the tether. In our courtyard, we lay out the basins and cloths and Daddy's kit.

"You'll feel sad, later," Daddy says, hesitating. "It's all right to feel sad."

"Why will I?"

He sits back on his heels, my daddy, to consider the question. He scratches his freckled forehead with a finger and smiles at me with his sad grey eyes. "Because it's cute," he says finally.

He has the lamb's neck pinned with a casual hand. Its eyeball is straining and rolling, and it's wheezing. Its tongue is a leathery grey. I pet its head to calm it. Daddy shifts his grip to the jaw. I put my little hand over his big hand and we slit its throat quick and deep. When it's bled out into the basin, Daddy asks me where I'd like to start.

"The legs are in the way," I say, so we start there.

"What am I going to do with you?" Daddy says in the middle of the dissection, looking at my hands all bloody, at the blood streaking my face. We've disjointed a leg and I'm making it flex by pulling the tendon. He's holding an eyeball between two fingers, gingerly.

We grin at each other.

"Little miss clever fingers," Herpyllis says from the archway nearest the kitchen. She shifts sleeping Nico to her hip— Nico, her blood-son, my little half-brother—so she can pull a couch into the sun and watch. I remember when he was born, though Herpyllis says I was too young. I remember his wrinkly face and his grip on my finger. I remember kissing and kissing him, and crying when he cried. I would lean against Herpyllis's knee and open the front of my dress to nurse my doll, Pretty-Head, off my speck of a nipple, while Herpyllis

nursed Nico, one hand playing in my hair. I've been her daughter since I was four.

"I'll remind you of this the next time you tell me you're too
clumsy to weave," Herpyllis says.

I slop some meat into the bowl she's given us, spattering
droplets of blood onto my dress.

"Filthy child," she says. "Who's going to want to marry
you?"

"One of my students," Daddy says promptly. "When the
time comes. There won't be a problem."

From all over the world, students come to Daddy's school
here in Athens, the Lyceum. Kings send their sons; our own
Alexander belonged to Daddy, once. Some of them are
wealthy enough to please even Herpyllis. They will see my
worth, Daddy says.

"What is her worth, exactly?" Herpyllis is irritable now.
Carelessly, I've spattered blood on the lamb's wool, which she
wants for a tunic. She calls for water to soak it. Nico sighs dra-
matically in his sleep, flinging out a pudgy arm.

Daddy sits back on his heels, considering the question.
I make a face at Herpyllis, who makes one back. She tucks
Nico's arm in and he sighs again, more quietly.

"It's interesting." Daddy looks at Nico. "The face of a child
reflects the face of both parents. Perhaps the mind works simi-
larly? If both parents are clever, the offspring—"

Herpyllis harrumphs.

"Then, too, a philosopher might encourage her interests—"
Herpyllis yawns.

"Or not suppress them, at any rate."

"I'm not getting married," I say. Usually I'm content to listen to their conversations, but this one is irresistible.

"Of course not, chickpea," Herpyllis says immediately. "You're still my baby."

"Not for a long, long time," Daddy adds. They think I'm scared, and want to comfort me. "Years and years. Girls marry much too young, these days. We should emulate the Spartans. Seventeen, eighteen summers. The body must finish developing."

"I'm not getting married," I say again, happily. "May I keep the skull?"

"We'll boil it clean," Daddy says. "What will you do instead, then?"

"Be a teacher, like you."

Gravely, Daddy and Herpyllis agree this is an excellent ambition.

Tycho, our big slave, brings the bowl of water Herpyllis called for. I smile at him and he nods. He's my favourite. Last summer he taught me to suck mussels right from their shells, but Herpyllis reproved him. He understood: little girls reach an age when familiarity with slaves must end. She hadn't been unkind; she'd been a servant herself until Daddy chose her, after my mother died. She was harshest with me, about my manners and appearance and behaviour, and that was because she loved me so much.

I remember the feel of the mussels, plump and wet, and the salt tang. I sneak a lick of lamb's blood. It's still warm.

❧◎❧

"Daddy took the whole day away from his school for you," Herpyllis tells me later that afternoon, hacking with less precision at the parts we brought to her kitchen. She isn't displeased, though. We'll have a feast tonight, and soup for days. "You'll be keeping the bones, I suppose?"

Bones are an excellent puzzle, Daddy says. I can apply myself to them and not get bored for weeks. Daddy knows I get bored. Herpyllis knows, too, but her solutions are less interesting—embroidery, crafts.

At bedtime, Daddy comes to tuck me in. "All right, pet?" he asks.

I ask him if we can do a bird next.

"Of course." He sits down next to me. "A pigeon."

"And a bream."

"A cuttlefish."

"A snake."

"Oh, a snake," Daddy says. "I'd love to do a snake. Did you know, in Persia, they have snakes as thick as a man's leg?"

"On land, or in the water?"

We chat until Herpyllis puts her head around the door frame and tells Daddy I need my beauty sleep.

"Why?" I say. Daddy and Herpyllis laugh.

At the door, he hesitates. "What we did today," he says. "Even if you were allowed, the sanctuary isn't the place for that. You understand?"

"Why?"

His lips quirk. "Why do you think?"

I close my eyes and see the temple, the hush and the gloom and the long shafts of light with the dust motes turning in them, the piles of sacred offerings, the guttering flame, the smell of spice, the priest so cool and glorious in his robe. And outside, in the sanctuary, the stone face of the god, and the gangly-legged lamb led so simply to the feet of the statue.

"Herpyllis will always let you use the kitchen," comes my father's voice from far away. I don't open my eyes. In the sanctuary, the lamb's death is an ecstasy. The bones and the blood aren't specimens there; they're a mystery that doesn't need solving. I think of the sadness Daddy talked about, feel it rinse through me, but it's not for the lamb. It's the gods I feel sorry for. What must they think, that we opened an animal without them today? That we didn't invite them at all? I imagine their big, beautiful faces, suffused with pain. That little girl, that one right there: doesn't she love us? What are we going to do with her?

"She's crying," I hear Herpyllis say. "You horrible man. What have you done to her?"

Someone comes close with a lamp.

"Open your eyes, Pytho," Daddy says, but I keep them shut. I'm looking at the insides of my own eyelids now, all red and spidery. "Are you crying?"

"I'm sleeping."

I get a kiss on each cheek, Daddy's whiskers and Herpyllis's sweet scent. She stays after he leaves, sitting beside me on my bed. "You don't have to help him if it upsets you," she says.

"I want to."

"I know," she says.

I open my eyes.

"Who loves you, anyway?" she says.

"You do," I say.

She snuffs the lamp but doesn't move. We sit in the dark.

"The poor gods," I say, and then I bury my face in her lap and sob.

HERPYLLIS SCOFFS AT DADDY'S WORK, Daddy's students and the monthly symposium he hosts in our big room. His colleagues attend, plum students, politicians, artists, diplomats, magistrates, priests; Daddy's symposia are famous throughout the city.

The subject for this month is virtue. "Oh, *virtue*," she sniffs. "Freeloaders, the lot of them. Take this, will you, baby? I'm going to drop it."

We're in the kitchen, just back from the market. I take the package of honeycomb from her and set it on the table so she can unload the rest of our purchases. I've had a growth spurt and am a hair taller than her now, though still unripe, my chest almost as flat as a boy's. We'll spend the day in the kitchen with the slaves. In the evening we'll put on our finery and sit in Herpyllis's room, eating smaller dishes of what the men are having, and afterwards weaving. Their voices will drone through the walls, muffled, occasionally bubbling up in argument or laughter. Herpyllis will try to gossip, and I'll shush her so I can listen. Eventually she'll put her finger to her lips and lead me into the hall so I can hear properly. She'll stand there examining her nails and smoothing her eyebrows while I try to understand. When we hear them rise to leave we'll run, giggling, back to her room.

"I wonder if dogs are virtuous." I spill lentils out on a clean cloth and start picking them over before I put them back in the pot on the shelf. Herpyllis likes her kitchen just so. "A hunting dog, say. You could have one that's too angry and bites everything, and one that's too shy and won't chase, and then—"

"Soak some of those, will you? Enough for ten." She pushes a strand of hair back from her forehead. "And then one in the middle that's everything a dog should be. Yes, yes, I know. And a bean that's too wrinkled, and a bean that's still moist, and a bean in the middle that exemplifies everything a bean should be. Most noble, gracious, perfect bean. A virtuous bean."

"What!" Daddy stands in the kitchen doorway. "Are you laughing at me?"

"Yes," Herpyllis and I say together.

Daddy grabs Herpyllis by the hips from behind, and nuzzles the back of her neck. "Who said you could laugh at me?"

I slip to the doorway, trying not to look at them. The slaves have already fled. We all know they like it in the kitchen.

"Beans, eh?" Daddy says.

Herpyllis's eyes are closed; she's already melting against him. Daddy's eyes are open. He smiles at me, and I know he's thinking about beans.

The guests start arriving after sundown. Tycho greets them and sees to the horses. Nico and I stand just inside the door with Herpyllis and Daddy. Nico, at eight summers, isn't really old enough to sit with the men, but Daddy lets him so long as he doesn't try to speak. Usually he eats too many cakes and falls asleep on the floor.

"Shall we play tiles?" Herpyllis murmurs to me.

"I want to play tiles," Nico says.

"And miss Daddy's party?" Herpyllis says. "Silly boy. We can play tiles tomorrow."

Nico groans.

"I don't want to play, anyway," I say, trying to help. "I want to read."

Another guest arrives, a colleague of Daddy's from the other school, the Academy. Daddy went to that school himself, when he was a young man, and is always gracious to his rivals there, though afterwards he will shake his head and tell Herpyllis their best teachers are all dead and the place won't last long.

"It's going to be boring!" Nico says. The rival, Akakios, grins at Daddy.

"Very, very boring," Daddy says.

"I only came for the food," Akakios says.

"No!" Nico realizes they're laughing at him, and stomps off.

"He's just a lad still," Akakios says kindly, once Herpyllis has gone after him. "At his age, all I wanted to do was fish and climb trees."

"For me, it was swimming," Daddy says.

"And what about you, sweet?" Akakios says to me. "Puppies, is it? Kittens?"

"All kinds of animals, really," I say.

Daddy's lips twitch, as I intended. "And she's a great help around the house," he offers.

Akakios waves this away. "You should hear him brag about you," he tells me. "A better mind than many of his students, he says. Always got her nose in a book. Should have been a boy."

I look at Daddy, who nods, smiling, flushing a little. *Yes, I said that.* I flush a little myself, with pleasure.

"Bactria, eh?" Akakios says to Daddy, changing the subject. I know that this is the latest news to arrive from the army: the king is in Bactria, at the end of the known world, calling himself Shahanshah, King of Kings, and founding city after city named after himself. Iskenderun, Iskandariya, and now Kandahar, the latest. These days, people announce the king's exploits to Daddy as though he's responsible. Daddy was his tutor, long ago, when I was a baby. It's their way of reminding us we're Macedonian and they're not.

"Indeed," Daddy says. "He's become quite the geographer."

"But maybe not such a cartographer," Akakios says. "He seems to have lost his way home."

Herpyllis returns, mock-grim, shaking her head. "We'll have to have a tile marathon tonight," she tells me. "But only after Nico practises his reading. I told him you'd help him."

I don't stamp my foot, groan, roll my eyes or spit, but all three adults laugh anyway. "She shoots sparks, doesn't she?" Akakios says.

"She gets bored," Daddy says. "It's the female aspect of the mind, I think. I was never bored."

"No, no." Akakios taps his temple with his finger. "She's got a flame in there, but it needs fuel. I get bored all the time. With lazy students, especially. That's why I so look forward to these evenings. They feed me for days."

Daddy bows; he bows back. Herpyllis manages not to snort; I hear it distinctly. These evenings are the biggest expense the household has. "The brain needs food just like the tummy." Akakios addresses me. "Your father feeds us, body and soul."

"Pompous prick," Herpyllis says after we're in Nico's room. "He brings a bag so he can squirrel food away to take home with him."

"That's a compliment to your cooking." I'm pressing my ear to the wall.

"I'm bored," Nico says, pushing his tablet away. "I'm hungry."

"You could have eaten with the men."

"Shut up."

"You shut up," I say. Mimicking him, drawing out the whine: "I'm *hungry*."

"Well, I am!"

"You're defective," I say. "Why can't you read yet?"

"Reading's hard," Herpyllis says immediately. "Please, no more fighting. Shall we go to the kitchen and see what's there?"

We follow her into the courtyard. The men's voices are clearer here, and I hang back. Daddy's speaking. I look pleadingly at Herpyllis.

"We'll be in the kitchen," she whispers.

In the past, I'd stand in the courtyard, quietly listening; perhaps creep to the doorway of the big room and listen from behind the curtains; then run fleet as a little doe back to the kitchen at the first quiver of that curtain. But something about tonight, about Nico giving up his place, about Daddy saying I should have been a boy, about Akakios's kindness, and I find myself tripping with quite a clatter over a little table just outside the big room. A moment later the curtain wings aside and Daddy helps me up off the floor. Beyond, I can see all the men on their couches craning to see who it is.

"Please, Daddy," I whisper.

Then I'm sitting in the corner that should have been Nico's, near Daddy, feet tucked up under me. The men are bemused.

"Getting eccentric in your dotage," one of them calls to Daddy. "You want to watch that."

"The lad is prettier," one of them says.

"But the girl's brighter," Akakios says.

I keep my mouth shut, and am relieved when they return to their argument.

"You cannot possibly believe all that modern nonsense you spout," an old man says to Daddy. I recognize him: Krios, a senior administrator for the city, one of Daddy's most regular guests. "The virtues of oak trees and donkeys and the gods know what else. It's all nonsense and you know it. The gods give us virtue."

"They lead by their example?" Daddy says.

"Don't blaspheme," the old man says mildly, and I see that he is used to Daddy, and too smart to be goaded. That must be why Daddy likes him, despite his antiquated opinions. "They set a better example than you'd like to admit. They would under-stand the presence of little Athena over there better than most of our colleagues here tonight."

He means me.

"The gods value women. They understand the power of women." Krios nods, agreeing with himself. "In their world, the greatest women are a match for the greatest men. Thinkers, warriors, healers."

"In *their* world," someone says.

"Plato, my master, taught that this world is an echo or a shadow of the ideal," Daddy says. "I'm afraid, in *this* world, our specimens are of a different quality."

I give Daddy a look that makes the men laugh.

"Not you, pet," Daddy says. "I wasn't talking about you."

"You were, though, surely," Krios says. "No offence to you, little Athena. But if we follow your argument to its conclusion, where do we get? The greatest virtue consists in flourishing to the greatest of our capacities. If we're an oak seed, we are virtuous in our vegetable growth. If we're an ass, we are virtuous in the most flourishing performance of our asinine tasks."

"Carrying saddlebags, and braying, and so on," I say.

I've thrown a pebble in their pond. There's a ripple of meaningful silence, and then Krios bows slightly, acknowledging me. "And if we are human, we are most virtuous when we are flourishing to the fullest of our capacities, the greatest of these being the intellect. That's correct, isn't it, little Athena? That's what your father teaches?"

"It is."

"You've read your father's books, haven't you?"

"I have."

"Some of them," Daddy says.

"Do you have a favourite?"

I let my mind run ahead through the conversation to come. I can see it laid out like tiles, this game of conversation the men play. I could play this tile, or that one. Daddy clears his throat, and I know he's playing the same game. I glance at him and he winks. *Quickly, Pytho.*

"The *Metaphysics*," I say. "I like the books about animals, too, and the dissection drawings, but I can read the *Metaphysics* again and again and learn something every time." I could have named any number of his books, and sent the game in a different direction with each choice, but I know few of the men here tonight have made it to the end of the *Metaphysics*, because I've heard Daddy tell Theophrastos so.

"What sort of things do you learn from it?" Krios asks.

"I've learned about change," I say. "Change in space, and time, and substance. I've learned about motion. I've learned about the perfect and eternal being, what Daddy calls the unmoved mover."

"About god," Krios says.

"About god as a metaphysical necessity," I say. "Remote and oblivious and lost in contemplation."

"You *have* encouraged her to flourish," Krios says to Daddy.

"It's getting to be a problem," Daddy says.

When their laughter dies down, Krios says, "The question, then, is whether little Athena is unique, or whether she is an example of what many girls could be, if they were encouraged by such fathers."

"Is that the question?" Daddy says. "You've hijacked the evening, pet."

"I'm Daddy's shadow," I say, because I want to tell him I love him.

"A freak." A new voice: Akakios. "Oh, I don't mean that unkindly. But how could such a great man produce an ordinary child? The tallest mountains have the tallest shadows. She's not representative of her sex. She's the exception that proves the rule."

Daddy bows, acknowledging the compliment.

"If he's right, child, you're destined for loneliness," Krios says.

"Only in the company of women," Daddy says. "She'll be all right so long as she has books."

"You'll have to find a husband willing to supply her," Akakios says.

"*If* he's right," Krios repeats.

He looks at me, and I see him thinking, *Go on, little Athena.*

"How many of you have daughters?" I ask.

Again that silence as they absorb the sound of my voice.

"Many of us," Akakios says, when it becomes clear they're not going to offer a show of hands.

"Can they read books?" I ask. "Not just household accounts. I mean real books."

No reaction.

"Could they?" I ask. "If you tried to teach them? If an ass could read, would it be wrong to teach it?"

"Would it be wrong not to?" Krios says.

"Would the ass be worse off?" Akakios asks. "Would it be unhappy?"

"Ah," Daddy says. "*That's* the question."

※

"Did you like that, pet?" Daddy asks when the last guest is gone.

"Very much."

"Shall our subject be animals next time?"

"Yes, please."

"They liked you," Daddy says. "You made them think."

We pause at the door to my room. He kisses the top of my head.

"Will I be lonely?" I ask.

He smiles. "Of course," he says. "Does that frighten you?"

"Are you lonely?"

"Of course."

"But you have us."

"I do," he says. "I have Herpyllis for when I'm cold, and Nico for when I want to laugh. And I have you, Pytho."

I wait while he thinks.

"For when you want to remember Mummy," I supply, finally, to spare us both.

He looks surprised. "That, too," he says. "But I was going to say: I have you, my Pytho, for when I want to think about the future."

I go up on my tiptoes and kiss his cheek. He clears his throat and stalks off to his bed.

✺◉✺

Daddy is as good as his word, and soon Herpyllis is saying he's completely lost his reason. He arranges displays of skeletons in the big room and has Tycho stack crates of live specimens in the courtyard. It's Herpyllis's job to feed them, which means it's really Nico's and mine. Birds, lizards, frogs, rabbits, turtles, and a weasel Nico names Nipper.

"Well, don't keep sticking your fingers in." I squeeze his hand with a rag until the bleeding stops. "I wonder what he's going to do with them all."

"Dissect them, of course," Nico says.

"After he's finished, I mean."

Nico trickles some grain through the roof of the birdcage, startling the pigeons. "You're going to be soup, yes you are," he coos.

I squeeze a sponge over the frogs. Daddy says we have to keep them moist. "I wonder what Herpyllis will do with these?"

"Feed them to the dogs?"

"Feed them to Daddy's students." We giggle. "Roast frog with walnuts."

"Figs," Nico says. "I don't like walnuts. Hey, you're bleeding."

I wipe my hands on my dress. "That's yours."

"No, not there. At the back."

I twist my skirts around and see the red-brown stain.

"Mummy!" Nico hollers. "Pytho sat on something sharp."

"You great lump," I say. "It means I can have a baby now."

Nico giggles.

"Shut up," I say.

"You shut up. You need a man to have a baby. He has to stick his penis in your hole."

"Thank you, Nico," Herpyllis says, coming into the courtyard. She takes one look at me and sweeps me away to her room. "Almost thirteen summers," she says. "About time."

"I'm not getting married."

"Yes, you are." Herpyllis strips me and calls for a basin of water and clean rags. "It's straight from here to the temple. We've had a man waiting there all this past year. He's very ugly and he has very bad breath."

"Stop it."

"Well, of course you're not getting married yet." She shows me how to wind the rag around and tie it in place. "You know Daddy's views. Eighteen summers, at least. That's years and years away."

"That's ancient. Gaiane's the same age as me, and she's getting married this summer."

Herpyllis stops wringing out my bloody dress and puts her hands on her hips. "So now you *do* want to be married?"

"I didn't say that!"

"You want to argue with me, is what you want. Like every other girl your age wants to argue with her mother." I don't correct her.

The next morning Herpyllis hustles me off to the temple, with gold coins and a bottle of perfume and the good wine she was saving for Daddy's name day. Daddy frowns, but says nothing. Tycho follows a little way behind us, carrying a bag of my old toys. I wrote the dedication out myself:

> *At the time of her menarche, Pythias consecrates to Artemis*
> *the ball that she loved, the net that held her hair; and her*
> *dolls, as is fitting; Pythias the virgin, to the virgin goddess.*
> *In return, spread your hand over the daughter of Aristotle*
> *and watch piously over this pious girl.*

I had a little fight with Herpyllis this morning when I tried to keep back Pretty-Head. I don't play with her or sleep with her anymore, but my mother sewed her for me, embroidered tiny pink roses on the hem of her dress. I like to stare at the tiny complication of those roses and imagine my mother straining her eyes over the stitches. I don't really remember her, and what I do recall—a gruff woman with heavy brows and a harsh voice who carried me on her hip while she barked at everyone but me—I've been told is wrong. I don't care: I know what I know. Sometimes when I'm fierce with Nico I feel her in me, surging up, and I feel safe and strong.

Herpyllis won that fight, though. "I don't care," Herpyllis says now as we walk. "You don't skint the goddess. I knew a girl when I was young, her mother gave second-best oil, and she never had a child. Walk straight, Pytho. Everyone doesn't need to know."

"It feels like it's slipping."

"It's fine. You'll get used to it. Don't sit down, that's all, until we get home, and then it won't soak through your clothes. You have to rinse it right away and hang it to dry in your room so Daddy doesn't have to see it."

"I know."

"Listen, though." She stops in the road, puts her hands on my shoulders. "You have to thank the goddess properly. No mistakes. She'll know if you don't get it right."

I think of Daddy, his dry scepticism. "How will she?"

"She sees. Like Daddy, but without all the cutting."

I take the stopper from the perfume and sniff. "Oh, Herpyllis, no. This is your best."

"Yes, it is."

In the temple we make our offerings and pray. I do everything in the right order, and I can see Herpyllis is happy. But the ritual is one thing; my feelings are another. I find I can't be thankful for the mess coming out of me and the prospect of some pimply boy breathing his halitosis into my mouth, but I can think of Herpyllis giving up her nicest perfume on my account and find loving tears in myself that way. I kiss Pretty-Head and stroke the little stitches on her dress one last time, then lay her with the other offerings. Herpyllis kisses me when we're done, wipes her eyes and mine, and says nothing all the way home, but holds my hand in hers. Her joy spills into me. Borrowed joy, but genuine enough to please the goddess, I hope.

At home, a strange boy is rapping his knuckles on our gate. My age, roughly. He wears a pack. His feet are filthy and raw, but his clothes are decent enough.

"You have to knock harder than that," Herpyllis says. "How will we possibly hear you?"

He turns his startled face to hers. Black eyes, black hair, hurt mouth; the bruise is almost gone, but not the swelling. He looks at me.

"Fetch Daddy," Herpyllis says. Her voice has hardened almost imperceptibly; the boy won't have heard the difference. "Are you hungry?" she says.

"Yes."

Deep voice. Older than I thought, by a year or two; he's small for his age.

"Go," Herpyllis says, sharply now, because I haven't moved.

I come back with Daddy and an apple. Herpyllis is holding a letter. The boy takes the apple and looks at me again, nods. Daddy takes the letter and reads.

"And here I thought I knew all my cousins," he says after a while. "Well. Shall we go in?"

"No," Herpyllis says later that afternoon, for the twentieth or thirtieth time. "We don't have room. He'd have to sleep in the stables."

"He could share with Nico."

"Absolutely not. We know nothing about him."

"There's that empty room in the servants' wing."

"Which you use for specimens. Where would you like us to move those to?"

"Just think of him as a bigger specimen," I say.

"Now, now." Daddy stands up. "A little charity, please, both of you. Imagine yourselves in his situation, sent away from his family because they can't afford to keep him. Thrown on our mercy. He's probably terrified. Where is he now, in the kitchen? Send him to me when he wakes up."

"I've never seen anyone eat the core of an apple," I say to Herpyllis when Daddy's gone back to his room. The new boy's sleeping on a mat by the hearth; Nico's running wild somewhere with his friends, and doesn't know yet about his new brother. "Where did he come from, again?"

"Amphissa, he says."

"You don't like him."

"I don't trust him."

"Why not?"

She looks at me. "I have no idea."

"I like him," I say.

"I know, sweetheart." She stands and kisses the top of my head. "You hold on to that. I think he has a hard path ahead of him."

"Why?"

She ruffles my hair, and goes to start cleaning out the specimen room.

I go to the kitchen. He's awake on his mat, and his eyes flare when he sees me. He sits up. I ask him what happened to his mouth. He doesn't answer.

"What's your name?" he says. That unexpectedly deep voice again, music I'm still getting used to.

"Pythias."

"Your mother doesn't like me."

"She's not my mother. Are you hungry?"

"Starving."

I get bread and cheese from the shelf. "Does it hurt to chew?"

"A little. But the tooth is tightening up."

"Did it happen before you left, or on the way?"

He rips the crust off and leaves it on the plate. "Before," he says through a soft mouthful.

"What did you do?"

"Kissed a girl," he says. I laugh. He shakes his head without looking up from his plate.

"What's your name?" I ask.

"Jason," he says.

Daddy nicknames him Myrmex, Little Ant, for his black black hair and black black eyes and busy busy ways. Always this way and that, never sitting still. Daddy says he's bright. The letter says so, and over the next few days Daddy himself takes him for walks and plays tiles with him and asks him to help with his specimens and books. *Feeling him out*, he calls it. I watch from a distance. I don't think he's so bright as all that. His reading is halting and he can't do basic syllogisms. He gets bored even more quickly than I do. His main loves are horses and walking through the streets with Daddy, seeing the way people treat him. Behind Daddy's back he mocks him, to Nico and me, but in public he likes nothing better than Daddy's hand on his shoulder, Daddy's quiet word in his ear, while around him men and boys look enviously on. "My son," Daddy introduces him, from almost the beginning.

"Oh, you know Daddy." Herpyllis's dislike of the new boy has hardened into something they both have to peer through, like a piece of resin. "He'll get tired of him after a while. And he'll realize you're better with the books, baby."

"Meanwhile, I've nothing to read."

Herpyllis looks exasperated. "Just go knock on his door and ask."

"I can't. He says I have to stay away from his room until—"

Herpyllis looks blank for a moment, then her face clears. "The smell." She nods. "He doesn't like it on me, either. Never mind. You're almost done for this month. Has it changed colour yet?"

"It's darker."

Herpyllis nods. "And there's less blood, yes? There, you see. You've done very well for the first time. You haven't soiled yourself once."

That would be because I change the rag so often my room flutters like an aviary, laundry as birds. An awful thought hits me. "Do you suppose Myrmex smells it too?"

"He's young still. He probably won't know what it is."

At my friend Gaiane's house, we discuss my new brother over our looms. "*Who* is he, again?" she asks.

"The son of some distant cousin of Daddy's. They can't afford to keep him, but he's bright supposedly, so they thought Daddy might take him in and educate him."

"Supposedly?"

I yank at a thread and it snaps.

"Jealous."

"Yes," I say. "No. Not exactly. Only Daddy can't see anyone else, at the moment. He's convinced Myrmex will run the school one day."

"What about Nico?"

"Nico's not clever enough."

"You are."

"I'm a girl. A bleeder."

"It's not all bad," Gaiane says. "You can get sick now, you know." She sets her wool down and looks at me. "Wandering womb, it's called. It gets you out of all kinds of things. You can get tired, dizzy, breathless, hysterical. Whatever you like, really. It's your womb migrating through your body, searching for moisture."

I raise my eyebrows.

"Really," she says.

Gaiane's mother, gauzy and fragrant, drifts in to check on us. "It's so nice to have you here, Pythias," she says. "It seems we hardly ever see you anymore. Gaiane's always saying how much she misses you." She leans over Gaiane's shoulder, inspects her work, and kisses her hair. When she looks at my loom, her eyebrows go up.

"Daddy's been teaching me—" I decide not to finish the sentence.

"Not weaving, he hasn't." She picks at my work, trying to correct it. "You should come here more often." I understand this is criticism of Herpyllis, whom she never mentions by name. Gaiane's parents are wealthy, citizens. Herpyllis, once a servant, has never been to their house.

"Pythias started her bleeding," Gaiane tells her mother. "And she has a new brother."

"Oh!" Her mother colours. "I didn't know—" Her fingers drift through the air, alluding.

"Herpyllis wasn't pregnant," I say. They both flinch; the word is for animals. *Expecting*, I should have said, or *blessed*. "A cousin has come to live with us."

"A cuckoo in the nest," Gaiane says.

"Has Gaiane told you about the wedding plans?" Her mother rises. "I'll have them bring you some juice. It's so hot, isn't it? Gaiane can tell you all about it."

"I've offended your mother," I say after she's gone.

"Mummy lives on a cloud," Gaiane says. "She just floats along. She's never trusted you since that time she caught you teaching me the alphabet. Is he handsome?"

I bite a thread with my teeth. "Who?"

"The cuckoo, of course."

Gaiane affects her mother's sweet vagueness, but she has a sharp streak that keeps us friends. Sharpness and lust; she's told me frankly she can't wait to be married, though she pretends to be frightened, like any well-brought-up girl.

"I don't know," I say honestly.

"Do you like him?"

"I feel sorry for him. I don't think he's used to people being nice to him. When he showed up on our doorstep, his face was all bruised."

"Has he tried to touch you?"

"No. Herpyllis keeps asking me that, too."

"Too bad for you." She's told me her betrothed can't keep his hands to himself. "Well, if his being here means you have less time with your father and more time for us, then I'm all for it."

I say something nice back, like *me too*.

When I get home, Herpyllis takes one look at my face and says, "That was a normal girl's day. Get used to it."

"Where's Daddy?"

"At the school."

"Where's Nico?"

"With him."

"Where's Myrmex?"

She shrugs, meaning *with them too, obviously*.

"Daddy usually waits for me on the days I visit Gaiane," I say. "Why didn't he wait for me?"

Her look says, *Pytho, don't*.

I help her in the kitchen, getting ready for tomorrow's symposium. I don't slam the knives around or anything. I don't make the chicken feet do a little dance or ask to keep the beak. When the men get home, Daddy goes straight to his work-room. I follow him there. "I have a headache," he says.

"I'll make you a poultice."

"No, that's all right. You go eat with the others." He touches his forehead with his fingertips, here and there, experimentally.

"Gaiane's mother has invited me to go weaving with them again tomorrow. I don't want to go."

"Pythias, please."

"Herpyllis will make me."

"It's very stuffy in here."

"I'm not bleeding anymore."

"Pythias, *please.*"

The next night, the night of Daddy's animal symposium, Myrmex is in my corner in the big room and I'm at Gaiane's house, where her mother has set her loom up next to mine. "Now, let's start simply, shall we?" she says. "It seems tricky to start, but you'll get the hang of it. You need a decent teacher, that's all."

"Is it stuffy in here?" I hold the back of my hand to my forehead and weave my head a little. "Maybe I should lie down."

Before I've even finished speaking, Gaiane's mother nods, smiles gently, and says, *Nice try.*

I should hate Myrmex. I try. The next morning I cut him dead.

"Hey," he says. "Hey, Pytho!"

He follows me out to the garden, where I commence pinching blossoms off the quince tree so the remaining fruit will thrive.

"What did I do?" he says.

I give him a look.

"They talked about you last night," he says.

I'm not asking I'm not asking I'm not asking.

"Pytho," he says, laughing. "Don't sulk."

I ignore him.

"Akakios made your father angry," he says. "He was talking about—oh, what was it? Something about plants. The difference between women and plants. Or there was no difference."

"The nutritive faculty versus the intellectual faculty," I say.

He laughs again. "You were listening!"

"I was at Gaiane's. Weaving."

"Ha," Myrmex says.

I punch him. Then we're rolling on the ground, wrestling. He's stronger, but I have no honour. I kick and bite and scratch. "You don't even care," I hiss. "You're stupid and you can't read and you might as well be a plant yourself. That party was *mine*."

"Stop." He tries to pin my hands, but I bite his shoulder and he yelps. I sense someone coming, someone big and quiet. I free a hand and manage to stick my finger in his eye and my thumb in his mouth and yank. He bites my thumb, hard, and then big hands lift me by my armpits, clean into the air.

Tycho.

"Young master," he says. "Young lady."

Myrmex's eye is red and weeping. My thumb is bleeding.

"What did Akakios say?" I ask.

"I'm blinded," Myrmex says.

Tycho puts me on the ground. "What did he say?" I demand.

"He said plants were vivified by the presence of the gods in them, and they died when the gods withdrew."

"That's dumb," I say. "What about a tree with one dead branch?"

"That's what your father said."

Tycho goes back in the house.

"Lookit," I say, and show him the ring of teeth marks at the base of my thumb.

He takes my hand and licks the blood off with his warm tongue. "Sorry."

"Sorry about your eye."

"Sorry about your symposium."

"You're not sorry."

"Well, I wouldn't rather be weaving," he says. "But I guess I'd rather be doing something else. Getting out into the city, that's what I'd like. Seeing the world."

"Daddy will let you," I say. "But you have to go to his parties. You'll hurt his feelings if you don't. Plus then you can tell me about them."

"You're weird," he says.

The bite marks will scar into a ring of white crescents around the joint.

⁂

Myrmex settles into the household. Herpyllis never warms to him. Daddy seems to pity him. Nico is afraid of his bullying. The servants treat him as a guest. But he and I, he and I. I've never held a person's weakness in my cupped hands, the way I feel I do his. Weakness and secrets: his loneliness, his hurt, his fear, his ordinary brain. He brings the world to me in pieces, the world I'm now shut out of: conversations he doesn't understand, specimens he can't name, manuscripts Daddy has set him to read that he can't make head or tail of. He even gets to attend classes at Daddy's school. I walk him through it all and help earn him Daddy's gruff love. In return, he teaches me to ride a horse and fake a fever and gamble at dice. I'm afraid for him, afraid of where he'd be without me to guide him. It's quite a responsibility.

THE KING IS DYING; THE KING DIES; THE KING IS DEAD. I walk down to the shore to watch the gulls squabble over this morsel. At sixteen summers, I shouldn't be going about alone. The trick is not to ask. Myrmex used to be my chaperone, but lately he fancies himself a strongman: hanging around the garrison, drinking with the soldiers, missing his classes with Daddy. He resents every minute he spends with the family. He carries a knife of extravagant length and detailing, paid for the gods know how. He still isn't much taller than me. He's always hefting things, trying to build up his arms. Daddy says this is a temporary infatuation, and will pass when he realizes fighting is intellectually unsatisfying.

I miss him, badly. I miss my friend, my brother. Lately, too, I miss the smell of him, and his snub nose and honey mouth and voice, the man who isn't my brother. I think it's his absence; if he were around more, things would go back to the way they were. Temporary infatuation, indeed.

I've brought the lentil pot just to have a reason to detour through the market and hear the gossip. Milk, cheese, olives, bread, nuts, herbs, fish, fruit, meat. High summer, the fat season. I wear a new muslin dress and veil and drift, listening. I feel pretty. *Babylon*, I hear. I know Babylon from Daddy's maps. *A headache, a massive headache.* Can you die of that? I don't ask it aloud, don't have to. *No, it was the guts. He was in agony for a day and a night and then he died. They buried him there. No, they're bringing him home. No, they were all wrong. He was alive. It was the double who'd died. They had a double who looked like him and appeared in public in his place. Assassins wouldn't know the difference. Poison, it was poison, but it was the double who'd died. Not the king. Not yet.*

"Now, beauty," the lentil seller says. "Red or green?"

I'm not a beauty, but I go to him in particular to hear the lie. I put the heavy pot on his table. "Green, please."

"Lucky lentils," he calls as he pours. "Favourite of the king."

Laughter all around us, not kind. Why? But of course I know why. Athenians can remember the time before Macedon, the time when they were independent and powerful and glorious in their own right. It's living memory; Daddy himself saw the battle where the king cut Athens down. They grumble and chafe and snigger and sneer, and fail to notice the Macedonian girl with the Athenian accent who understands more about democracy and empire than they ever will.

The pot's heavy; I balance it on my hip like the servant women do. I want to buy a bird, too, feeling momentousness in the air, but Herpyllis is possessive of the marketing and will find something wrong with it. I can do the heavy pots, but the party pieces she likes to save for herself.

The walk to the beach is long with the pot denting my hip. Tycho wants to carry it, but he already has the towels and lunch and waterskins and my books. We scramble over the hot rocks, away from the popular swimming spots, until we find a deserted scythe of sand at the bottom of a steep rock-dislodging scramble, sheltered by cliffs, with a little sea cave for privacy. I undress and dive into the water while Tycho sinks sticks in the sand and arranges a little oilskin tent for me. When I come out the lentil pot has disappeared, probably into his pack. He's put my food on plates, poured me a cup of water, and arranged my books in the tent, then gone to sit some distance away on the rocks, staring out to sea.

I eat and drink and pick at the blister from the lentil pot puffing on my palm. I build an obstacle course for the thumb-nail-sized crab I've brought up from the water's edge and watch him negotiate sand hummocks and rivulets of my drinking water. Once I look for Tycho and see him down at the water-line, picking shells from the kelp and sucking them out. Every now and then he splashes water on his bristly skull, cooling off.

Late in the afternoon, we pack for home. My palm's seep-ing a little and I don't ask for the pot. We stop by Gaiane's house for a visit, but the slave who goes to her room to announce me returns saying she's indisposed. She's never turned me away before. But two babies in the four years since her mar-riage, one stillbirth, and pregnant again; *indisposed*. I don't think anything of it.

Sure enough, Herpyllis has felt the turbulence as I have, in the cooking part of her brain, and has bought a pheasant on her own trip to the market. Nico, twelve summers now, is in the courtyard playing Greeks and Persians with the tail feathers. Herpyllis and I make a walnut sauce.

"Do you think it's true?" she asks me, pausing the pestle.

Tycho appears at that moment to set the lentil pot just inside the kitchen doorway. I lift it to its place on the shelf.

"Yes," I say. "I think it's true."

Herpyllis shakes her head, blinking hard.

At supper, when Daddy asks me how I spent my day, I tell him some of what I heard. Some, not all. I don't tell him about the laughter.

"Never mind, pet," he says. "He's died at least a dozen times in the last year. He'll die a few more before we need to start paying attention."

Still, his long fingers fidget with a napkin. He's a bad liar but a good worrier. If he really thought the rumour were true, there'd be tears. All the same, he doesn't like to think of it; it upsets him. He was once like a father to the king, long ago, or so he likes to claim. Herpyllis is glaring at me for upsetting him.

"There was a nice breeze by the sea," I say. "Cooler than in town. We should take a picnic sometime." Her glare softens. "Just the four of us." She smiles. "We could take the cart. Spend the day."

My little brother groans.

"Absolutely not," Daddy says. "Rattle my bones loose. I ache enough as it is. Do you want to finish me?"

Herpyllis immediately does a switchback. "You could have thought of that yourself," she says to me. "You know your father hates the seaside."

"Since when?" I say.

"Why don't we eat cat?" Nico asks. Sweet, worried clown. I love his furrowed face. He holds something up on a knife. "Is this cat? It tastes like cat."

"Daddy loves the seaside," I say. "We all do."

"I have gills," Daddy confirms. He frowns at Nico's knife. "It looks stringy enough for cat." Nico giggles, but Daddy's eyes wander away and grow troubled. "Likely I'll never see the sea again," he says to none of us. He's been saying things like this more and more lately, since he passed his sixtieth summer. The number bothers him.

"What does cat taste like?" I ask Nico.

He chews chews chews gulps, dead pleased. "Sweet and salty at the same time."

"Disgusting child." Herpyllis reaches over to wipe gravy from his cheek. "You know perfectly well it's pheasant." They have the same dark hair and green eyes, the same too-wide smile. I take after my own dead mother: lighter curls, deeper voice. I have our father's eyes, though, that clear unlovely grey. Thinking is unlovely on a girl, Herpyllis has told me, though she likes to fix my hair and kiss my cheek when I'll let her. She says kissing is good for the skin.

"Never again," Daddy says again, a little sharper this time.

I reach across the table to squeeze his freckled, paper-skinned hand. "One day the sea will get tired of waiting and come to you. It'll suck itself up into one big wave and come rolling across Athens until it reaches you. It'll say, *Where have you been?*"

"Will it bring specimens?" Daddy says. "I haven't looked at new marine specimens in so long. I used to take the king looking for specimens, when he was just a boy. Did I ever tell you how I taught him to swim? He was afraid until I taught him."

"The king was never afraid," Nico says.

Daddy leans forward. "He tried not to show it, but I knew. Have I never told you that story?"

Herpyllis and I look at each other. Her lips quirk ever so slightly. I have to look away so I won't smile.

Daddy tells Nico for the fortieth or fiftieth time how he taught the king to open his eyes underwater, a skill my brother and I have had since babyhood. "It is impossible for sea water to hurt the eyes," Daddy says. "Your eyes already contain salt water. You've tasted your tears, haven't you?"

Nico nods. Daddy often encouraged us to poke and taste and smell our various excretions, to learn about the workings of our bodies. "Why does the sea sting, then?"

"Algae, perhaps," Daddy says. "Tiny bits of it. Pythias?"

"Daddy?"

"You'll stay home tomorrow, please, and help me with my books."

A job I like, the periodic tidying of his library, and the glimpse of books I'm not normally allowed to see. Plus he likes to talk about his work at such times, and show me his collections and drawings.

"Well, I'm going hunting," my brother says. He's recently made himself a lot of equipment: bow and arrows, a fishing rod, and a stick lashed to a flint blade for a spear. He and his friends set out every morning insisting it'll be rabbit for supper.

"No," Daddy says. "You'll help too. We're all staying home tomorrow."

Nico looks at Herpyllis with do-something eyes. She opens her mouth to speak when we hear loud laughter from outside the front gate. Male, more than one. A moment's quiet, the sound of a flute, then more laughter. We hear them move off down the street, singing. *Calliope's daughter, Calliope's daughter. . .*

"Drunks," Daddy says. "No, sit down. You don't need to go look."

My brother sits back down and starts hacking at the remains on his plate. He's sulking. Suddenly he yelps. He's cut himself, drawing a bead of blood above one knuckle, black in the lamplight.

"Let me see." I make a tourniquet with my napkin and hold it tight until the bleeding is staunched. Daddy's taught me everything he knows about doctoring. I can splint a sprain, lance an abscess, bring down a fever, probably even deliver a baby. He's shown me his tools and described the process. I kiss the tip of Nico's finger and wipe pain-tears from his cheeks with my thumbs. "Stupid boy."

"Stop it," he says. "Stop treating me like a baby."

Daddy pushes his plate away. "The Athenians don't know what's good for them. I'll speak to the king when he comes home, explain the situation. If he spent more time here, if they got to know him—"

Daddy and the king haven't spoken since Nico was born, when the army left Pella and we came to Athens.

"I'll write him tomorrow," Daddy says. "The army will take it in dispatches. They know who I am."

Nico yawns. Herpyllis starts clearing the table, sorting what she can save for soup, scraping our plates onto hers.

"May I go to the garrison with you when you deliver it?" I ask. "I haven't seen Myrmex in days."

"No," Daddy says.

The next morning there's a pile of excrement in front of our gate and more daubed on our outside walls. Tycho and another of our slaves, Pyrrhaios, set grimly to work cleaning it off.

"Dog *and* cow," Nico says. "Man, too." He went to see; I wasn't allowed. The stench in our yard is everything the drunks intended. Daddy has been in his library since before dawn, Herpyllis says; he's slept poorly for years. He's told her he's working—probably on his letter to the king—and will call us when he's ready for our help. We don't know if he's smelled the insult.

Herpyllis sits in the inner courtyard, fiercely carding wool. Nico and I fence for a while with the pheasant feathers and then Herpyllis calls me over to do my hair. She has pins and combs and jewels and all kinds of whatnot. A long session then, to soothe her. I sit at her feet while she complains about the crunchy effect of salt water on my hair. She says she's going to speak to Tycho. "You shouldn't be traipsing around the beaches all by yourself, anyway. He should know better."

"How's he going to stop me?" I pick up a clip set with seashells, lovely tiny blue-brown speckled dove shells.

She snatches it from my hand. "I'll stop you," she says.

I smile to infuriate her. I'm my father's child. I do what I want.

"I'll speak to your father." She yanks and yanks again harder when I don't show hurt. "He doesn't always remember you're a girl, that's his problem. Well, who can blame him? Look at you. Have you once used that kohl I got you?"

"Once," I say.

"*And* your clothes are always dirty. You look like a goose-girl just in from the yard."

"It's only dust." I lick my thumb and rub a brown spot clear on my grey-brown foot. My hems are a little ratty, it's true.

"You should be in linen. Silk. A daughter of mine." She sticks the comb in her mouth and executes something complicated with my curls and a gold clip in the shape of a bee, one of her own. She takes the comb out, frowns, and thumbs my eyebrows smooth. "Daughter of mine."

Pyrrhaios appears in the archway that separates the inner yard from the outer, where we keep the horses. "Lady," he says.

I stand. Herpyllis gathers the hair things into her basket.

"A visitor, Lady."

"Who is it?"

"Master Theophrastos, Lady."

Herpyllis follows me to the outer yard, where Theophrastos is pacing. When he sees us, his face contorts.

"Fetch your master," Herpyllis tells Pyrrhaios. She touches his hand and he goes.

"Uncle," I say, and hug him. He's hugely tall and when I hug him my head fits comfortably in the hollow of his chest. In the past I've felt the life in him against my belly, but this time he stays soft. His shoulders shake. He lets me go and takes my face in his hands. I echo the gesture, and thumb the tears away as I did with Nico just last night. "So it's true?"

He blinks. I let him go and Herpyllis takes my place, hugging his tall skinny self, the tree-like length of him. He pats her back and kisses the top of her head but his eyes find mine. "Your father?"

"He doesn't know."

Herpyllis lifts her face from his chest and I see she's crying too. "It's *not* true," she says. "It's not."

I look at the packed earth of the yard, the clean sky, the gate.

"What's not true?" Daddy comes stomping into the yard, his old-man stomp, with Pyrrhaios behind him. He looks from face to face. "What's happened?"

"The gate's open," I say.

Herpyllis throws her veil over her face, squats, and starts to rock, keening softly.

"Gods' sake," Daddy says. He looks annoyed. "I'm trying to work."

"He's dead," Theophrastos says.

The earth, the sky.

Daddy looks at me.

"The gate's open," I say. "We should close it."

Daddy nods at Tycho, who's come in from his cleaning. He closes the main gate behind him.

"We should lock it."

"Shut your mouth," Daddy says to me, and then he starts to sob.

※

Theophrastos stays the night, although his house is only a short walk from ours. At first my fears are justified: we can hear the uproar from the city, farther and nearer and farther again, and see elegant spires of smoke rising from different districts. Once our front gate is fiercely rattled, but by the time Pyrrhaios gets to the yard, whoever tested it is gone. By nightfall we can hear music and smell smoke and roasting meat on the breeze. Parties, then; celebrations. I intuit Myrmex is out there somewhere, drinking and carousing, the party mattering more than the reason for it. Shame stops us eating, speaking, until well after dark. Daddy, Theophrastos and I lie on couches in the courtyard. Herpyllis returns from putting Nico to bed with a tray of bread and pickings from last night's bird. Her eyes look poached. Theophrastos is rolling and unrolling a set of scrolls on his lap, not reading. Daddy stares into nothing.

I make room on my couch for Herpyllis.

"Their own king," Daddy says. "They're turning on him that fast."

"They never loved him." Theophrastos puts the scrolls aside and reaches for food. He makes up a plate, not a scant one, and I'm just having thoughts about his ability to eat at a time like this when he sets it beside Daddy. Daddy looks disgusted.

"Please, Master," Theophrastos says.

When I was a baby, he was Daddy's student; now he teaches with Daddy at the school and will head it one day, Herpyllis says. His name used to be Tyrtamos, but Daddy changed it to Theophrastos because of his divine eloquence. I'm unfamiliar with his divine eloquence because I'm not allowed to attend classes. He's so tall and thin and mild and affable. He loves Daddy like a father and Nico like a little brother. He told Herpyllis once that I laugh too loudly.

Daddy had another pet before Theophrastos, a man named Callisthenes. Well, I don't remember him. He went East with the army and got locked in a cage for disobedience and died.

Daddy says Callisthenes needed a spur but Theophrastos needs a bridle. Theophrastos keeps the botanical garden at the school and curates the museum specimens. He knows a lot of collectors and has acquired my father's gift for talking to people who know more than he does and writing down what they say. I shift on my couch, reaching forward for a bite of something, far enough to see that the scrolls in his lap are in his own hand.

"Thirty-two summers," Daddy says of the king.

"We die just when we are beginning to live," Theophrastos says.

Daddy grunts and starts to pick at the plate. Herpyllis pours the men watered wine, us water. They dip their bread in saucers of olive oil and bowls of salt. There are apricots in the kitchen, but they're probably too happy a fruit for the moment. Herpyllis doesn't eat so I don't either, even though I'm hungry. I should probably try to cry. Nico cried. That's why he's in bed already: exhausted by grief.

"We'll leave the city, of course," Daddy says.

"That's probably wise." Theophrastos takes a last piece of bread to wipe the grease from his fingers, then drops it on his plate. "Just until they get the vengefulness out of them. A few days by the sea until the fuss dies down. A week or two, maybe? The girls will enjoy a holiday."

"Nico, too," Herpyllis says.

"He's a grand boy." Theophrastos pulls his scrolls back into his lap. "How about you, Pythias? Who'll miss you if you're gone a few days? I bet there's someone."

Apricots, lovely apricots.

"Leave her alone," Herpyllis says. "She's my good girl."

"We'll be foreigners here until we die," Daddy says. "No Athenian would have her. She's Macedon-born. She can't breed a citizen. We should probably just go home."

A curious silence.

"Athens is home," Herpyllis says.

"Athens is home to Athenians. We're Macedonian."

"Athens *is* Macedonian. Alexander's death doesn't change that." They look at me because I said the words aloud. *Alexander's death.*

"Antipater is still regent," Theophrastos says. "Pythias is right about that. You have powerful friends still. This outburst"—he waves a hand to indicate the sounds of singing and drunkenness that waft in from all sides—"this isn't rebellion. It's a little release, a little letting-off of old feelings, old desires. Athens is in no real position to overthrow Macedonian rule. Those days are over."

"They pleasure themselves tonight," Herpyllis says bitterly. "And they'll be spent in the morning."

"That's enough." Daddy squeezes his eyes shut and opens them looking confused, like he can't focus. "I'm a symbol. A known associate of the king. They'll kill me just as soon as they think they can get away with it. Look at Socrates."

We all look at Daddy.

"They made him drink hemlock for corrupting the youth of Athens. They kill philosophers," Daddy says, slowly and loudly, like we're all stupid. "Athenians kill philosophers." He stands. Slowly, painfully, with great nobility. "I love my king," he says hoarsely. "I am loyal to my king. We leave."

Herpyllis rises abruptly, loads the tray with our plates, and goes to the kitchen.

"Sounion," I say.

"What's that?" Daddy says.

"We could go to Sounion."

Theophrastos smiles bemusedly, as he always does when I have an opinion. *If a cat could speak*, he asked me once, *what* *would it say?*

*I don't know*, I answered. *I'm a dog.*

"Whyever?" Theophrastos says now.

"It's close," I say. "No hard journey for Daddy. And it's on the sea."

"And," Daddy says.

"It's beautiful."

"And."

"And the Macedonian fleet is there."

"Good girl," he says. "However, Chalcis is better."

"It's farther."

"And less beautiful. But it has a full garrison, and I have property there. The farm."

"Chalcis," I say. "We need to tell Myrmex."

"Myrmex is fine," Daddy says.

I raise my eyebrows.

"He sent word," Daddy says. "He got trapped on the other side of the city when the riots started. He's staying with Akakios. You remember Akakios. He'll be home in a few days, when it's safe."

I see Akakios walking slowly through the streets with Myrmex, his hand on my brother's shoulder the way Daddy used to do, speaking thoughtfully to him while around them the party continues. I see them stop at a stall to buy meat skewers and bread, then walk on, enjoying the festive night, talking about the nutritive faculty.

The next morning, Theophrastos gives my father gifts: some books he's been working on. "Something new for the journey," he says to Daddy. "This is a bibliography I've been assembling. I'm rather proud of it, actually, how much I've done these last few years. When you look at it all together like that. And then this one—"

"Ah," Daddy says. "Your plants."

"My plants," Theophrastos says.

We will see him again before we go; it's arranged. We'll visit the school in a day or so, and Daddy will give him final instructions.

"Not final," Theophrastos says. "A few weeks, maximum. Will you bring Nico?"

"If he'll come."

When he's gone and the gate is bolted behind him, Daddy says to me, "Come on. Let's take a look at these."

We go to his study and sit side by side, looking through the bibliography.

"*Juices, Complexions, and Flesh,*" Daddy reads.

"*On Honey,*" I read.

"*Animals That Live In Holes.*"

"*The Difference of the Voices of Similar Animals.*"

"Look," Daddy says. "He's written one on hair, one on tyranny, and three on water."

"*Political, Ethical, Physical, and Amatory Problems.*"

"Amatory problems," Daddy snorts, and we laugh until our guts ache. It's the first time we've laughed in days.

Herpyllis says when a man is at ease his testicles are tender, but when he's excited they go wizened and tight. I don't know if she's trying to give me the world or take it away.

I watch her now, standing in the courtyard next to my father as he explains the move to the assembled household, Tycho and Simon and the rest of them. Her eyes find our big slave, Pyrrhaios, then the ground.

"I will not pretend that this move will be easy," my father is saying. "I will not pretend that our life in Chalcis will be better. I'm confident it will be worse. But our way of life here is over now. We are not wanted in Athens anymore. I am not wanted. My loyalty to my student—"

His chest heaves, but he collects himself.

"We leave the day after tomorrow. Pack only what you cannot leave behind. Your mistress will instruct you about the household goods. Now, as for food. My own requirements are minimal, as you all know—"

While he drones on, I watch Simon and Tycho exchange glances. They are my father's best oxen, and they know the greatest burden will fall on them. The women have started to weep, and Olympios's child is gumming dirt again. It's a filthy little thing. Nico stands as tall as he can, listening as a soldier to his general.

Myrmex still isn't home.

I hatch a little egg of a plan: I'll take it upon myself to speak with every member of the household privately, to assure them that the move is only temporary and we'll be back in

Athens by the apple-picking. It would be natural for me to enquire after Myrmex in such a context. Even to visit his room. To penetrate his thick, hot, sour, salty-smelling room.

I start with my little brother.

"You don't pack like that, silly," I tell him. "Those'll break. You need some thorny burnet to wrap around each of them. There are lots of bushes on the road to the market. It's springy when it's dry. It'll protect them."

He puts down the little clay lion and deer and bear he's had since he was a baby. *Splotch* falls the first tear, darkening the lion's back.

"You're too old for toys, anyway," I say, ruffling his hair.

"They're not toys," he says. "They're keepsakes."

Next I visit the servants, starting with Simon and his wife, Thale. I find them in the storeroom, arguing. They stop when they see me. Simon of the yellow teeth and grey grizzlature around the muzzle; Thale the barren with her mouse-coloured eyes and greasy grey curls pinned tight to her scalp.

"Don't be frightened," I tell them. "It won't be for long." Speechless, they look at me, then at each other. I'm pleased at the effect of my words and drift away, running a finger along a shelf as I go.

Pyrrhaios is in the stables, mucking out. I've had reason to watch him lately and I lean in the doorway for a while now, silently. I've seen Herpyllis do the same. His torso is as articulated as a beetle's, I'll give her that.

"Missed some," I say finally, pointing at the straw.

He starts. "You, is it? How long have you been there?"

I say my bit about the move to Chalcis being only temporary.

"That's not what your father says."

"My father is a great man with many worries."

He laughs.

Next the other slaves: Tycho, Philo, Olympios, his toddler, and Ambracis. I find black-eyed Ambracis first, in the kitchen, chopping vegetables. She's not much older than me. She listens staring at her hands and when I'm finished says, "Yes, Lady."

"You may look at me, girl," I say.

She looks at my chin.

"Have you been crying?"

"Onions, Lady."

I look at her chopping board and see the clutter of onions. I feel a bit silly then. I find I can't ask about Myrmex while I'm feeling silly.

Olympios and Philo are in the courtyard with the toddler: clever Olympios is mending a leather harness with an enormous needle and a length of sinew; thick-witted Philo is turning carrot scrapings into the compost. The child, tethered by the waist to a column, is whining after a ball that's rolled just out of its reach. When I nudge it back with my toe the child squints up at me, little crab-hands pinching for my dress. I step back out of reach.

"Lady," the men say.

"Her face is dirty," I say. "She needs a wipe." Before either of them react I go to the barrel and dip the hem of my dress. Holding it bunched into an ear, I approach the child, who coos. I squat in front of it and wipe at the dirt and food and nose-pick on its face. It plucks at my hands, trying to get my rings.

"You must keep her clean," I tell Olympios. "She will have better health if you keep her clean. My father teaches this to his students."

Olympios bows. "Most gracious lady."

Olympios got the child on another of our slaves, who died during the birth the spring before last. My father said we were not to be angry. They did as animals do, he said, experiencing coolness and heat according to the seasons, and should not be punished for the demands of their animal natures, which were utterly involuntary. The girl was a loss, certainly, but the baby would have value one day.

How cold that sounds! In fact Herpyllis and I both wept for the girl, and Herpyllis took it on herself to find a wet nurse. The house was sombre until the baby learned to smile, at about forty days. Nowadays the toddler is mostly Ambracis's charge, though Olympios is unusually attached to it and likes to work near it when he can. We all find this endearing. My father is not a cold man, and we all take pride in the reputation of our house for indulgence to the slaves. We're known for it, for many streets around.

"Do you have questions about the trip to Chalcis?" I ask now.

His eyes stray to the child.

"Of course," I say. "We wouldn't leave her."

"Thank you, Lady."

"That's very good work, Philo," I say, and he beams. He smacks the compost a few more times with the fork, patting it down. "Ambracis probably has some more scraps for you in the kitchen." He trots off, happily. He's cheerful and good for heavy work, even if he doesn't talk much. He likes to keep near Olympios and the child.

"Where is, where is—Tycho?" I ask. *Tycho*, I think to myself. *Who cares where Tycho is?*

"Master sent him on errands. Arranging for carts, I think."

I stop myself from thanking him. I do yank a ring I've grown tired of from my finger, a cockleshell on a plain gold band, and drop it in the child's lap on my way out of the yard. It shrieks with pleasure.

I detour through the men's quarters on the way to my own room just to breathe the air, the hot leather smell.

"No," my father says, seeing the veil I've put on as he passes from his study to his bedroom, where the pot is. A trip he makes a couple of times an hour, every hour.

"Please," I say.

"No."

I take the veil off, ball it up, and throw it on the ground. Housebound, then, I must wait for Tycho, pacing up and down the yard where everyone can see me.

"Do you need something to do?" Herpyllis calls from her room.

"No!"

Nico passes by me and walks straight out of the gate. An hour later he's back with a sack of burnet. He shows it to me for approval.

"Bring everything out here," I say.

We're rolling and tying the last of his toys in the springy dried bushes, which leave long fine scratches on our hands, when Tycho returns. "I'll bring you a crate, young master," he says to Nico.

I follow him inside, to the pantry. "Why isn't Myrmex home yet?" I ask, when everyone else is out of earshot.

He shakes his head.

"Has Daddy not told him we're going?"

He looks at my face. "I'll see to it he knows."

"I could write a letter for you to take to Akakios. This afternoon?"

He removes some jars of oil from a small crate and shakes his head. "Master has jobs for me this afternoon. Let me give this to the young master and I'll go do it now."

"A very quick letter."

He bows. I follow him back to the courtyard, intending to run to my room for paper and ink, but he gives Nico the crate and is gone through the gate before I can stop him. *Oh.*

Herpyllis has closed her door, which is unusual. I can't think why she would be changing her clothes before lunch. Though if she's going out, maybe she'll take me. I hesitate, wondering whether to knock.

"Come in, and close the door behind you, Pytho," she calls. My baby name.

Her room is dark. The curtains are drawn and she's lit just one single-wick lamp. She's sitting cross-legged on the floor, her back to the door, busy with something in her lap.

"How did you know it was me?"

"Close the door," she says again.

I close it.

"I always know when it's you," she says. "I feel the fuss in the air, like a storm coming, and I smell the wild lavender that grows by the sea."

She smiles at me over her shoulder and I stick my tongue out at her. "What are you doing?"

She pats the ground beside her and I sit. She's braiding something.

"Don't you want more light?"

She shakes her head. "Your father doesn't like me doing this. It's quickly done and then he doesn't need to know. Want to help?"

I recognize it now: an iunx. She's using various threads and hairs, probably sneaked from each of us, and cups of milk, honey, and water, and a little mound of spices in the charred saucer she uses for burning.

"To protect us on our journey," she says.

I get up. "Of course I don't want to help," I say. "If my father disapproves, then so do I. That's just superstition."

"La, la, la," Herpyllis says. "I can't hear you. Shall we go out? I need some laurel to finish this. We can go to the grove near your father's school."

"Daddy won't let us."

Herpyllis draws a tiny knot tight and clips a loose end expertly with her teeth. "He can't say no if we don't ask him." She filches something fine off her tongue, looks at it, and flicks it onto the floor. "Nico will chaperone us, and Pyrrhaios will come too. We'll be perfectly safe."

"Don't expect me to do any picking."

"Of course not. You'd spoil it anyway with your unpleasantness. The leaves would shrivel in your hands."

"That's right," I say.

"Shrivel and catch fire, probably," Herpyllis says. "I could teach you so much, you know, but you're a stubborn nut."

"That's right," I say again, and skip back to my room to retrieve my veil, grateful as a dog for its walk.

❦

On our too-brief walk this afternoon, I got my own sackful of burnet. Despite her show of nonchalance, Herpyllis took care to have us all back far too soon. I've laid out what I want to bring on my bed. Herpyllis, passing my open doorway, rolls her eyes. "Gods," she says, but she's too busy to interfere. She and Ambracis ripped the kitchen apart after we got back this afternoon, and they're working on the linens now. We leave tomorrow morning.

First are Daddy's old surgical tools, inherited from *his* father: pipes, probes, needles, knives, spoons, forceps, clamps, extraction hooks and the enormous vaginal dilator I've always loved for its great complicated importance. Daddy gave me the whole lot to play with long ago, saying he had no use for them anymore. They take a whole crate to themselves. Next comes my mother. She's resting at the moment, but when the time comes we'll have her ashes exhumed to be mingled with Daddy's. I keep ready an unusually small, beautiful funerary urn. Daddy said my mother loved small things, which was why he chose that particular urn. The image on it is of a mother and a little girl, who is me. I'll carry the urn on my lap until it's safely in my new room in Chalcis.

All that remains are my clothes and jewels, which I dump into the trunk at the end of my bed. I'll strip the bed linens in the morning. My collections of shells and rocks and bird skeletons and pressed wildflowers can all wait here until we return. I remember to add the little pot of kohl Herpyllis gave me; she'll notice if I leave it behind by-accident-on-purpose.

"Pytho, help!" she calls now.

I find her in the storeroom with Ambracis and Thale, all three of them sweating and dusty and struggling to hold up one end of a shelf that's somehow ripped off the wall. They're up to their ankles in shards of pottery and an explosion of dried beans. I unload the remaining pots so they can safely lower the shelf, and offer to fetch the broom and pan.

"Look in Myrmex's room," Herpyllis says. "I was sweeping there before this."

Myrmex's room smells of leather and horses and something else, something I don't know. I wonder if I've left a thread of my wild lavender smell for him.

After the cleaning of the beans and the cramming of the carts, we sit in the courtyard drinking a tonic before bed to help us sleep. Nico and I don't often get wine.

"Nicomachos and I will visit the school in the morning while you finish packing," Daddy tells Herpyllis. "I have some last instructions for Theophrastos. You'll have the carts ready in the street, please, so we can set off once we've returned."

"Take Pythias, too." Herpyllis leans forward to refill our glasses. "She'll just mooch about and get under my feet."

"Mooch," Nico says, giggling.

Herpyllis takes his glass and pours his wine into her own.

"What about Myrmex?"

Daddy and Herpyllis look at me.

"We can't just leave him," I say.

Daddy and Herpyllis look at each other. "He's been told," she says.

"Pretty one." Daddy moves to my couch to put his arm around my shoulders. "We all love him. But he's grown now. Soon he's going to start making his own decisions. Maybe even tomorrow."

"Not tomorrow," I say. Daddy holds me while I sob. When I lift my face from his shoulder, I see Herpyllis is pouring my wine into hers, too.

"Come with us tomorrow, then, pet," Daddy says. "If it'll make you feel better."

I nod, and snuffle, and feel for the pouch I've hidden under my dress at my waist. It contains the black hairs I picked from Myrmex's fur blanket before Herpyllis called to ask what was taking me so long with the broom.

Apollo of the Twilight stands just inside the gates of Daddy's school. He rests one forearm on the top of his head, like Daddy when he's frazzled and trying to think, as he leans on a tree trunk. His marble hair is braided like a child's, though he's taller than Theophrastos.

We're in our heavy travelling clothes, the clothes we'll be sleeping in tonight, and I've borrowed Herpyllis's finest muslin veil. Daddy walks ahead, saying many serious things to Theophrastos, who listens attentively, and to Nico, who does not. I trail behind. Dragonflies, poppies, tiny dandelions, light purple iris, snail shells bleached white in death. Curious looks my way.

I worked it out last night in bed. It's been four years since I was last here, ten minutes' walk from our house.

I pick up a snail shell and a small white stone to put in my pouch, later, when I can get under my dress.

Men are coming up to Daddy, touching him, hugging him, wiping away tears. Daddy looks tired. I know it's the effort of not crying himself. I slip up quietly so he can feel me near. "Pythias?" he says, starting.

I blush under my veil as the men look politely away from me, from this gross breach of my modesty: the public utterance of my name.

"So like your mother, for a moment." He touches my cheek through the cloth. "I mistook you."

I go up on my toes to whisper in his ear that I need to sit down. He looks relieved. We go into one of the lecture halls, where Theophrastos has had a table laid with food and drink. Daddy settles onto his couch with a pained groan while his students assemble around him. I whisper to Theophrastos that we might send word to Herpyllis to have the carts brought here so he won't have to walk home again. He nods. Libations, blessings, valedictory speeches.

"I'm bored," Nico murmurs to me. We're at the back of the room, out of the way, supervised by Theophrastos.

"I wonder if they do this every time he goes on holiday," I say.

"Shh." Theophrastos frowns: sternly at me, cross-eyed at Nico.

"I've been enjoying the book you gave Daddy," I whisper. "On botany."

"Ah," he says.

"The part on medicinal herbs especially," I whisper. "I was wondering—"

"It's hard to hear you in here," Theophrastos says. "Perhaps it's better if you don't try to talk."

I bow my head obediently. I've had my fun with him, anyway.

When it's time to leave, I touch Daddy's arm.

"All right, pet," he says. "It's all right. Don't be frightened. Don't be sad."

I whisper in his ear to speed us along, to spare him.

"My daughter is unwell." His voice is loud, hoarse. The men part for us.

The carts are indeed waiting in the street, loaded with our goods and our people. Simon holding the horses; Herpyllis in the first cart; Thale dandling the child; Pyrrhaios, Olympios, Philo, and Ambracis holding Philo's hand so he won't wander away; Tycho; and—leaning against the last cart—Apollo of the Twilight himself, but loose-curled, chewing on half a smile.

"Too much sun and standing," Daddy diagnoses, as many hands reach to catch me and my weak knees.

He makes me wait. He walks at the end of our caravan with Pyrrhaios. Guarding us, oh yes. Knowing he's with us, I can ignore him for the moment. The streets are busy, busier than usual, with a lot of doorway loitering and dart-eyed muttering and finger pointing. Daddy is famous. But then someone calls

"Macedonians," and "fucking Macedonians" again from another part of the street, and then a chorus of voices call other words—Herpyllis claps her hands over my ears. The cart speeds up, the horses rump-smacked by Simon, and I'm thinking of Gaiane, and I'm understanding why she wouldn't see me, or was told not to. Daddy's face is white. He takes Nico's hand in one of his and mine in the other, and sits as tall as he can.

The stone hits him in the side of the head and bounces back onto the road. A small stone. Daddy drops my hand to swat at the place, as though at a bug, and then touches his temple with his fingertips, feeling the blood there.

Myrmex is beside us now, knife drawn. Oh, he's fierce! He's shouting all kinds of things, but Herpyllis, behind me, is wiggling her fingers so hard in my ears, I can't make out a thing. Pyrrhaios is on the other side of our cart too, suddenly, saying something to Herpyllis. She pops her fingers out of my ears and wipes them reflexively on her lap. "Stand up," she tells me and Nico.

Another stone rebounds off Daddy's shoulder.

"Stand up, babies," she says. "Let them see who they're hurting."

We stand. I have to set my legs wide to balance on the bumping cart. I feel a tug at my back and air on my face and understand: Herpyllis has pulled my veil off. I take Nico's hand and close my eyes, waiting for the bite of a stone on my face or breasts, but nothing happens. We ride like that, standing, me with my eyes closed, until we leave the shouting behind.

"Sit, now," Herpyllis says.

We're in a quieter street, closer to the outskirts of the city. Daddy is lying in the bottom of the carts on a pile of skins. His entire face is an apology. I shake my head: *It's not your fault.*

"You see," he says. "I wasn't wrong."

Myrmex climbs up beside me.

"That was magnificent," he says, and then I want it to happen all over again.

We sit for a long time shoulder to shoulder, hip to hip. He pulls my veil back on himself and spends a couple of moments arranging the muslin with his fine fingers. I want to rest my head on his shoulder, as Nico rests on Herpyllis, but that might be less than magnificent, so I hold myself nobly upright instead. He keeps a hand on his knife and scans the landscape like an eagle. Gods, we are a pair!

The journey to Chalcis takes two days. We pass the first night in a field, sleeping in the carts. Herpyllis and I have a cart to ourselves, and Tycho rigs up an oilskin tent over us as he did for me at the beach. We eat Herpyllis's picnic—bread and cheese and fruit and nuts—and we each get another tonic. I read by lamplight while she tidies the camp, but I put the book away when she returns.

"What is it?" she asks.

"Poetry."

She nods, lies back, and stares at the roof of our tent. "Read me some?"

"How's Nico?"

"He's being brave. Daddy's with him. He'll sleep, I think."

"You won't?"

"Probably not." She smiles tiredly; more warmly when I meet her eyes. "It'll be good to get to Chalcis. You were brave yourself, today."

"I wasn't."

"I don't think any of us expected it to be like this."

"Daddy did, I guess."

She shrugs. "We're so used to thinking we're smarter than the smartest man in the world. Because he can never find his bath oils, or remember your friends' names. Maybe we should give him a little more credit."

I lean over to kiss her cheek.

"Read me some," she says. "There's still oil in the lamp, and I'm wide awake."

I pull the book back out and find one of my favourites, the one about the temple by the clear water where sleep comes dropping through the apple branches.

"Louder," Daddy's voice calls from the next cart, and Nico calls "Louder, Pytho."

I hesitate.

"Pytho?" Myrmex calls sleepily.

"'Deathless Aphrodite of the spangled mind,'" I begin.

The next morning dawns pink and hot. We take turns peeing in the barley, and Herpyllis hands out apricots and sticky sesame cake to eat as we ride. The land is flat, rich, ringed by mountains; we're riding across the bottom of a vast green-gold cup. By noon, my head is throbbing and I throw up over the side of the cart. Tycho puts the tent back up. Even though it's stifling under the oilskin, Daddy says I'm sun-sick and need the shade. He makes everyone else wear hats, except Myrmex, who refuses. He's distant again today, maybe because he saw my sick-up. I'm so disgusting. I ruin everything.

We arrive in Chalcis by late afternoon. We pass gravestones along the road leading into the west side of town, and convoys of Macedonian soldiers moving to and from the garrison. They ignore us, which isn't bad. I'm sitting up by now, taking sips from the cup Herpyllis holds for me, trying to get something back inside me and keep it down.

The town straddles an isthmus that splits it neatly into two halves, like an apple. On the west side, the mainland side, the garrison dominates, set on a rocky rise. The slopes are treed with olive and cypress, and there are some nice houses set in a collar at the bottom of the hill. Officers' residences, probably. East, across the strait—forty paces or so at its narrowest—is the town proper, bustling with shops and workshops and temples and the market and smaller houses. Outside the town on the east side is Euboia, the very best farmland in the world. That's where Daddy's property is.

An hour ago, Daddy sent Pyrrhaios ahead on our best horse, Frost, named for her white socks. Now, as we arrive at the gate at the base of the road that leads up to the garrison, we're met by an officer maybe half Daddy's age. Clearly a Macedonian: he styles himself like Alexander, short hair and clean-shaven. Daddy looks pleased. "Thaulos is the leader of the garrison," he murmurs to Herpyllis. "He knows who I am."

Thaulos looks harassed and exhausted, and greets Daddy by saying, "Is it true?"

Daddy hesitates.

"They celebrate his death?"

Daddy puts his hands on the man's shoulders and shakes his head, meaning *yes*.

Thaulos squeezes his eyes shut and starts to sob. "They should be celebrating his return."

"We've come for sanctuary," Daddy says. "I wrote to you. Did you not get my letter? Is the house not prepared?"

"The house," Thaulos repeats. He looks at the rest of us, briefly, and back to my father. "The house?"

"You will see to it," Daddy says. He's gone pale again.

Thaulos hesitates, gives a curt nod. Then we're jerking slowly, painfully up the hill. The gates clang closed behind us. At the top of the hill, through another gate, he leads us to a corner of a busy courtyard just inside the walls.

"You can bivouac here tonight," Thaulos says. "Cook fires over there. Tomorrow you'll have to be out. We've got reinforcements coming. We'll need every available space."

"The house," Daddy says.

"Later," Thaulos says. He seems angry now, perhaps because we saw him cry. Slowly we all dismount, stretching our jarred, aching bodies. I whisper to Herpyllis. "I'll find us a pot," she whispers back. "We can do it in the tent."

Daddy announces he's going for a walk, as though he needs to stretch his legs after a morning's work, and simply walks away.

"Go after him," Herpyllis whispers to Pyrrhaios.

Pyrrhaios follows him at a discreet distance, leaving the rest of us to set up a makeshift camp in as small a space as possible. The shadows are already lengthening and it's too late to market. Herpyllis's picnic has run out, and she looks like she's going to cry.

Tycho whips the tent up for us and we take our turns with the pot.

"How much money have we got?" I whisper to Herpyllis when she emerges, with that grim but collected look that means success, hard-earned, in the nethers.

"A fair bit," she murmurs. "Daddy gave me all the coin in the house. It's in the bag with the salt fish."

We approach Myrmex together and explain our plan. Herpyllis gives him the leather pouch and tells him how much more to promise once the deal is made. Surprisingly he offers no argument—Myrmex always wants to put his own spin on things, add his own flair—and leaves in the direction of the officers' quarters.

He returns long after Daddy is back, long after midnight, and Daddy and Nico and the servants are all asleep and Herpyllis and I have snuffed our lamp so no one will realize we're still awake. We hear him trip over something and giggle.

"So?" She sticks her head out through the tent door, clearly startling him; he lurches heavily against the side of the cart and giggles again. The horses, tethered nearby, shuffle, disturbed.

"All taken care of." He waves at her like he's leaving on a long journey, lies down in the dust beside the embers of our cook-fire, and is snoring before she has had time to refasten the flap.

A particularly emphatic clanging of cook-pots just outside our tent wakens me. I wish I could swim back under. Herpyllis, beside me, snuffles gently on. I imagine insomniac Daddy already off on one of his walks, and Nico rabbit-eyed in the tent in the next cart, waiting for one of us to get him.

There is scrabbling at our tent door. I whip Herpyllis's dress—the nearest thing to hand—over my face. Through the muslin I see Myrmex's unshaven face poke through the opening. "Boo."

I take the dress back off. "How's your head?"

He makes a face, then crawls in on his elbows. "Mommy still sleeping?"

"Yes," Herpyllis says, without opening her eyes.

"I found us a house."

How I love his bleary, blood-shot eyes, his awful stubbly cheeks, his dirty fingernails, his feral smell. Nico can wait a little longer. I stretch, tousle my hair to try and fluff it up a little, wonder about the propriety of sitting up with just a blanket covering my little chest. He's my brother too, after all, just like Nico. Somewhat like Nico.

Something metal raps on the side of our cart. Herpyllis's eyes pop open and Myrmex wriggles backwards, disappearing. "You need to move this," a voice says.

Then we are working fast—dressing in our smelly travel-stained clothes for the third day, throwing everything into the carts, while Myrmex helps Tycho hitch the horses. Herpyllis goes straight to Nico, who lets her hug him. Daddy and

Pyrrhaios, as I'd guessed, are gone. Around us, soldiers wait impatiently. They arrived in the night and have been assigned our place in the camp; they want us out, now. I get busy reloading the sacks and crates we piled on the ground to make room for sleeping, and trip over a tent peg already staked by a soldier who's tired of waiting for us. "Move that," he says to Myrmex, meaning me.

Once we're back in the carts and rolling, Herpyllis leans over to Myrmex. "Where are we going?" she whispers. He pretends he doesn't hear.

Soldiers open the gates for us and suddenly we're out of the garrison and on the dirt track that leads down the hill. It's early still, the sun fingering almost horizontally through the pine and cypress. All around us songbirds are bubbling. I repeat Herpyllis's question aloud.

"I told you, I got us a house," Myrmex says.

"But how will Daddy know where we're—"

"Daddy," Myrmex says. "Daddy, daddy, daddy."

At the bottom of the hill, we bear left. The houses here are a mishmash of huts and villas crowded around the base of the hill. Above them is a tonsured strip where the trees were removed beneath the garrison walls. Myrmex looks deadly pleased with himself. We pull to a stop in front of a villa slightly more secluded than the others, set vertiginously beneath the garrison walls and veiled by a stand of cypress as tall as a man on another's shoulders. A poised, expectant silence.

"What have you done?" Herpyllis says. "We can't afford this."

Myrmex's face registers surprise like pain.

Daddy appears in the doorway, stooping beneath the trailing ivy that's encroaching on the front of the house. "We'll need to cut this back," he calls. "What do you think?"

Herpyllis eases down off the cart. "Whose is this?"

"Ours," Daddy says.

"We can't afford this." She looks angry.

"Whose is it really?" I murmur.

"Don't think about it," Myrmex says.

Nico launches from the cart like a Myrmidon storming the beach at Troy. A puppy, a fuzzy golden thing, peers out from behind Daddy's ankles. Recognizing one of his own, he muddles forward to greet Nico, tongue flopping amiably.

"Comes with the house," Myrmex says, and in his pride I see a boy like Nico and a puppy, too. I shouldn't be able to see these things, but I do. That's what Herpyllis means when she says I'm not attractive.

"Thank you," I say to Myrmex, since no one else will.

"I won it at dice."

"Oh, you did not."

"I sort of did." Myrmex thinks for a minute, frowning. "I can't really remember, actually. It's ours, though."

I want to ask where the person he won it from will live now, and about the money Herpyllis and I gave him, but he holds his hand out to ease me down from the cart and his touch wipes my mind clean.

"The grand tour," Daddy says, ushering Herpyllis and me inside.

The house is confusing. It's bigger than it looks from outside, and the rooms don't seem to stay still; we pop in and out of doors, finding and losing each other, laughing at closets that lead to rooms and private courtyards that seem utterly soundproof. I feel like Herpyllis has given me a tonic. I finally find the room I want for myself, the one with butterflies painted on the walls, but when I call out for them to come see, no one can hear me. I wonder again about who lived here before us, for what girl these butterflies were painted, and if she hates me now.

The grounds, too, are deceptively large and secluded; the whole property is walled, including the fruit trees and out-buildings, and by the large kitchen garden is a second dwelling, a liveable shed I intuit Myrmex will claim.

We settle in, which takes less time than the packing did. I find small, curious clues around the house: a wet wine-cup under a couch (but how is it still wet?); sweet green grapes, still dew-bejewelled, in a bowl on the kitchen table; a mattress still warm to the touch, as though someone just rose from it, on the bed that will be mine.

"I think you like it here," Daddy says, startling me. I had lain down just for a minute on the warm mattress and drifted off.

"Do you?"

He looks straight at me, his eyes unexpectedly clear, the haze of worry and self-absorption momentarily lifted. "It's not home."

"It is if we decide it is."

He leans down to press a kiss on my hair.

In the afternoon, Herpyllis says she wants a walk into town. "We'll all go," Daddy says. His clarity has persisted, translating into a rare good humour through lunch (fresh bread from the larder—*how?*—and a salad from the garden). He arm-wrestled Nico, patted the puppy, even put an arm around Myrmex's shoulders and told him he'd done well. Myrmex blushed.

We walk away from the residences clustered at the base of the hill, while Daddy explains that the tonsured strip at the top is to prevent anyone from scaling the cliffs, and that the residents of our neighbourhood are largely Macedonian, and feel safer in the shadow of the army. The huts, he explains, were cobbled together by poor refugees, whom we should treat kindly should we encounter them. He says the word "refugees" as though it has nothing to do with us.

We stand for a while at the isthmus, watching the tide funnel through the narrowest point, then pay a man to raft us across. "Euboia," Daddy announces grandly on the other side, as though he owns the whole island. In the town proper, we visit the market. Here Daddy is whimsical, buying fish and pomegranates and cumin seed and squash flowers, imagining the ridiculous dishes Herpyllis will make of them for our supper that evening. She rolls her eyes. He buys a fishing stick for Nico and promises to take him; a vial of scented oil for Herpyllis; and a woollen cloak for Myrmex, a reward for securing the house. "And what would Pythias like?" he asks.

I shake my head. It's a happy day, but money remains a worry, surely, and Myrmex's cloak cost more than a book.

"You're a fortunate man." A large hand descends on my shoulder, squeezing. "A girl who refuses gifts. I should be so lucky in my own daughters."

"She is utterly modest," Daddy says happily. "If only I could stop her eating, I could bring her upkeep down to nothing."

The big man laughs. I take myself out from under his hand and duck under Daddy's wing, pretending shyness, so I can get a look at him.

"I know who you are," the big man says to Daddy. "Word of your coming preceded you. We're honoured, honoured, to have you among us. This is your child?"

"My child," Daddy agrees. Herpyllis and Nico hang back, far enough that the man probably doesn't know we're together. Daddy ignores them. Myrmex, browsing the stalls, hasn't noticed.

"Plios." The man claps Daddy on the shoulder. "I'm the magistrate. On my way to the courts as we speak. When did you arrive?"

"Last night."

"Perfect timing." The magistrate claps Daddy's back again, making him stagger-step. "My eldest girl is getting married day after tomorrow. We're having an informal supper before the wedding so the women can come too. You'll join us, yes? I'll have you first that way. You'll offend me if you say no." He rubs his hands together. "A coup for me! And you'll bring your lovely, modest daughter? You can meet everyone who matters."

Daddy accepts. They exchange compliments, and the man pinches my cheek through my veil before he leaves.

"That's excellent," Daddy says. He seems unsure. He touches his temple with his fingertips, like there's a pain budding there. I exchange looks with Herpyllis, who's stepped forward again.

"Daddy's tired," I whisper to Herpyllis. "We should head back."

Herpyllis says nothing, but stalks off ahead of us, dragging Nico by the hand. Myrmex glances over, sees us leaving, and waves.

"Do you have anything to wear for a party?" Daddy asks.

"Anything to *wear?*" I look at him like he's turned into a cuttlefish.

"Girls like new clothes for parties." He says this like it's a fundamental proposition. *All x is y. No a is b. Girls like new clothes for parties.* "I'll send Herpyllis with you tomorrow to choose something."

*That'll be fun*, I don't say, reading jealousy in the fierce line of her spine.

At the isthmus, Daddy tugs my hand, bringing me to a stop. "Notice anything?"

I look down at the raft, up at the garrison, down at the water. I look again.

"Good girl," Daddy says.

"But it's backwards. An hour ago it flowed that way"— I point north—"and now it's running that way." I point south.

"A switchback tide." Daddy looks like Nico with the puppy. "Chalcis is famous for it. The current changes direction at the turn of the tide."

"I don't understand."

He hesitates. Then murmurs, "Neither do I."
Puts his finger to his lips; winks.

❧

A thousand lamps send golden tongues licking in all the secret places. The air smells minglingly of meat and flowers and a loosening perfume that makes my thinking vague and my free hand unable to make a fist. The house of Plios is dazzling by twilight, scented and flickering and pretty to the ears, even, with flute girls and a blind drummer and wind chimes made of cockleshells, and the voices of men and women drinking, affectionate, old friends at ease. Daddy holds my other hand tightly, and moves through the room like a ship, parting the company in stately splendour and leaving a froth of whispers in his wake. My famous daddy! My first party! A kindly woman, her hair spangled with hammered gold flowers, hands me a cup and folds my veil back for me so I won't have to let go of Daddy's hand. "You're among friends, dear," she says, eyes crinkling. She touches a fingertip to her tongue and smoothes my eyebrows, then turns away. I take tiny sips of the sweet drink and watch the women's jewellery on the plates and shelves of their various bosoms: necklaces of gold flowers and seed pods, insects, shell-shapes, and spiral loopings of gold wire. I sip again—tiny, tiny sips—and smile shyly at Daddy. He is splendid tonight in snow-white wool, hair neatly trimmed, clean-shaven in the Macedonian style, ears and nostrils plucked hairless by Herpyllis.

She brought me home a dress from the market, thinking to

deprive me of the pleasure of choosing it, and dressed me herself. I'm wearing a girdle at my waist, my first, and my breasts are
bound, and my hair is up. She yanked my hair hard, mumbling
bitterly about the expense of new clothes through a mouthful of
pins. But she took care that I should look perfect and expensive,
as befitted our house, and kissed me before we left, carefully,
because I had powder on my cheeks and the famous kohl on my
eyes. I'd done that myself, to surprise her; she'd wiped it off
with spit on a cloth and redone it to her own satisfaction.

"Daughter."

I snap back from the contemplation of my odd-looking
self in a bronze to smile at the introductions Daddy's making.
Plios pinches my cheek again and says I'm as pretty as he'd
guessed. The woman who gave me the drink is back for formal
introductions. Glycera is her name, and these are her daughters,
three beauties in soft colours who don't speak, but smile without malice at everyone and everything. Thaulos is here, and
greets my father more warmly than he did on the hill; a priestess of Artemis—white-haired, with black brows—is presented
to us; also a handsome officer. I can't hear clearly over the tin-
kling music, and decide it's time to stop sipping. Daddy is
bragging about me. "Reads, writes, keeps the kitchen garden,"
he's saying to Glycera. "Knows her herbs. She healed one of
our slaves last winter of an infection, all by herself, no fuss.
Didn't tell anybody. Lanced the abscess, cleaned it, applied a
hot fennel poultice, checked the pus for—"

"Daddy."

"The body is not disgusting," Daddy says, too loudly,
reproving. "As I was saying, the pus—"

"An accomplished young woman," Glycera says. "A credit to you, my dear." That stops Daddy. He's not used to being anyone's dear. "What else can she do?"

"Cauterize a cut, set a broken bone, apply leeches—"

"Weave," I say. "Embroider, a little."

"Does she sing?" the priestess wants to know.

"Like a hoopoe," I say.

The room bursts into laughter; everyone is listening.

"Dance?" Glycera asks.

Daddy frowns; I look at the floor.

"I think she loves flowers," the officer says. "I sense it. She fills the house with vases of wildflowers, beautifully arranged." I look at him gratefully. "Blue," he adds. His eyes crinkle too when he smiles, but not like Glycera's. He's young. "A bit of purple, but mostly blue."

His name is Euphranor. I ask one of Glycera's smiling daughters in the women's room, where the pots are. She smiles at the question, without curiosity; I wonder if she's drugged, though she checks her appearance carefully enough in the bronze, and corrects a smudge of colour on the lid of one eye with a steady finger. She smiles again when she sees me watching.

Back in the big room, Glycera takes my elbow. "I've offended your good father," she says. "Only I do so love dancing. My friends know this eccentricity of mine and forgive me. I'm sorry if I've shocked you. There's nothing so beautiful as a young girl dancing. So innocent. So healthy for the body. Do you enjoy exercise?"

"I swim," I admit. She covers her mouth with her hand and

her eyes go big. "Is that terrible?" I say, maybe a bit wistfully. "Will I not be allowed to swim here?"

"Utterly charming," Glycera says, which isn't an answer. She lifts my chin with a single finger and adds, "There. That's right. We wear our chins terribly high in Chalcis."

I giggle.

"Oh, we're going to be great friends." Glycera beams again. "You'll come weave with us, my daughters and me. We're a house full of women now that my dear husband is gone. Five years ago, now. We love sweet company. Anything you need, you call on me. You have no mother, I think."

"My mother died when I was three."

"Precious." Her eyes go bright and she pulls me to her, smothering me briefly in the front of her dress. "You come to us whenever you want." She glances over at Daddy, who's holding forth about something across the room. I see the men around him exchanging glances, amused at something Daddy isn't aware of. "They shouldn't laugh at him. He's a greater man than any of them will ever be," she says.

I feel surprise, and gratitude. "Will you excuse me?"

"You hold him up like a stake holds a vine. I see it. Go, go to him. You're everything to him; those men are less than nothing."

I go quickly to Daddy, slipping my hand in his.

"I was just explaining about the farm," he says. "Richest land in the world. I plan to take a much larger role in the running of it, now we're living here. I have some theories I intend to implement."

"Quite so," Plios says, loudly, patting his shoulder like he's stupid *and* deaf. "May I tempt you with a quince cake, little one?"

Before I can do anything to spare Daddy, the magistrate has led me away to a low table of food surrounded by rich-fabricked couches. "So much food." He shakes his head, gives me a plate, and takes one for himself. "You'll help me make a dent in it, won't you?"

I'm not used to eating in front of strangers. I take a few almonds, a few grapes. I expect Plios to make some joke, but he watches me gravely. I can see he's deciding something.

I wonder what grown women say to grown men. "Your house is beautiful." This sounds about right.

"It's yours," he says. "Open to you anytime, I mean. Is the villa terribly small, compared to what you had before? Are you comfortable there? I can send over whatever you need: servants, furniture. Say the word."

I thank him, tell him we're fine.

"Eat," he says. "I've embarrassed you. Eat your grapes. We help each other here, you'll see."

"Here you are." My father takes a couch and pats the spot next to him, bringing me close. I make a plate for him and he eats hungrily, cheese crumbling down his front, lips glistening with the oil he dipped his bread in. I catch his eye and touch my lips casually. He looks for a napkin.

Euphranor, the young officer, takes the couch next to ours. "I've been thinking about your farm." He pours a cup of wine and pushes it toward Daddy, across the low, food-laden table. "I could take you out there, if you like. You and your family. We could make a day of it, take a picnic. I have a small property close to where you describe. I wouldn't mind popping my head in on the way. In fact, I think we might even be neighbours. I'm terribly interested in the theories you plan to implement. Animal husbandry, is it? Crop rotation? Fertilizers?" I have to squeeze my lips together despite myself to contain a smile.

Then they're pouring the wine unwatered, and my eyes are closing, and the music is faster and louder, and it's time to go. I am pressed to chest after chest, and offers of help, anything we might need, are repeated in my ear. My great daddy is puffed up with wine and food and respect, and doesn't notice the criss-cross web of curious glances that weave around his head. Tycho, waiting at a distance to escort us, is holding an enormous basket.

๛

"So?" Herpyllis says. She must have heard our footsteps coming up the path, and is waiting in the doorway for us.

We follow Tycho to the kitchen, where he sets the basket on the table. Herpyllis unpacks eggs, cheese, cake, wine, cold pies, fruit. Daddy grunts, kisses her and then me, and wanders off—to bed, or to work. To his solitude, anyway. Herpyllis sorts grimly through the food, finally slamming a crock of soft cheese on the table and breathing deeply through her nose. "Charity," she says. Her kohled eyes are bright with hatred. She looks beautiful.

"I want to get this off." I wriggle inside my dress.

She follows me to the butterfly room and helps me with the unpinning, unwinding, unbinding, releasing of hair, washing of face, unlacing of tight sandals designed to emphasize the tininess of my not-so-tiny feet.

"Are you going to tell me about it?" she says finally.

So I tell her about the food, the music, the perfume, the people we met, the quality. I don't patronize her by pretending I didn't enjoy it. She listens, and asks the occasional question.

I see her struggling not to sneer or criticize.

"There was an officer named Euphranor. He offered to escort us to the farm, on a picnic."

She flinches slightly and looks at her lap.

"All of us," I say. "I told him all of us."

She looks up. "How did you do that?"

"I told him my father's companion was a mother to me, and I had a little brother who loves animals."

Her face scrolls through a series of emotions. Her eyes go wet.

"Stop it," I say.

"You don't understand." She wipes her eyes on her hem, leaving black streaks on the cloth. "I want all these things for you. Wine and perfume and gold and cavalry officers and—what—*cakes*." She takes both my hands in both of hers. "You're going to be gone so soon. They're going to take you from me."

"Never," I say.

"They'll take you into their world, and leave me behind in this one. Look at Myrmex."

"I'm not Myrmex," I say.

She falls asleep before I do, in my bed, curled on her side like a child, cheeks still wet, my arms around her like a mother's.

"Of course I'm coming," Myrmex says. "Why, wasn't I invited? You didn't mention me, maybe? The minor fact of my existence? Not worth mentioning?"

I open my mouth, but Myrmex is full of umbrage.

"You're ashamed of me, all of you. Well I *am* coming, and I'm going to chew with my mouth open and piss in the river and—"

"Enough," Daddy says.

"—*ask how much everything costs*," Myrmex hisses.

Daddy and Herpyllis and I burst out laughing.

"You can ride Pinch," Daddy says.

Myrmex hesitates. He loves Pinch.

"What about me?" Nico says. "Can I ride too?"

"It's a long way for the pony," Daddy says. "And we don't know the ground."

Nico looks stricken. "I already told him about the picnic. He wants to come."

I shake my hair down around my face like a mane, and snort, and say in a deep snuffling horse-voice, "I want to come."

Everyone laughs again, Myrmex too. "Go tell Tycho, then," Daddy says. "He'll get them ready."

"Rather Pyrrhaios, don't you think?" Herpyllis gets up and starts tidying the breakfast table. "He's better with the horses."

Soon we're gathered in front of the house: Myrmex on Pinch, Nico on Spiffy, Daddy on Frost, Herpyllis and me standing, big Pyrrhaios adjusting Nico's tack. The carts we hired to move are long gone, but Euphranor said he'd take care of everything; we weren't to bring a thing.

"You look like you're going to the theatre, not the farm!" Euphranor is suddenly just there, solidified from the shadows of the trees, with his eye-crinkling smile. "Beautiful family. Are you the one who likes animals?" This last to Nico, who's sitting painfully tall. Euphranor slaps Spiffy's neck affectionately. "You've got a fine friend here. We rarely get them this fine in the cavalry." Nico beams. "And who's this?" Euphranor smiles at Myrmex and scratches Pinch's nose.

"That's Pinch," Nico says, before Myrmex can reply.

For the rest of the day, Euphranor calls Myrmex Pinch.

He has a cart for Herpyllis and me lined with furs and purple silk cushions. He himself rides a black stallion, high-strung and fiery and snorting and head-tossing, mane like the sea and so on. Well. It's a very pretty animal, and Myrmex is very, very angry and can't do anything about it. He longs for everything Euphranor has, from his commission to his clothes to his height to his arrogance, and after the first few tongue-tied moments he can't go back and correct the mistake about his name without looking like a fool. He rides at the back of our caravan, fuming, on the horse he's now forced to hate.

The plan is to visit Euphranor's farm first—he's arranged lunch for us there—and then Daddy's property later in the afternoon. Euboia is farmland from a dream of farmland: green and golden, a long treed lane between endless fields, poppies in the ditches, birds in the branches, odd rambling houses made bigger generation after generation, each adding another room or two, all lovelied over with clematis and creeping grapevines. Chickens in the yards, dogs chasing us down the lane. We turn into Euphranor's property, where an old man steps from the shadow of a doorway to greet us. He has no teeth.

"Demetrios!" Euphranor greets him. "We thought we might swim."

"The pond's covered in scum." The old man rubs his hands. "Pollen scum. I'll give it a skim for you."

"No, don't bother." Euphranor claps his shoulder, squeezes. "Pinch here will do the honours. One mighty splash should clear it for the ladies, eh, Pinch?"

Myrmex looks at me.

"I thought we'd eat in the grove." Euphranor holds his hand out to assist Herpyllis from the cart, then me. The catch of his calluses. "Cooler there. A nap, a swim, whatever you like."

"I'd like to see your farm." Daddy's got himself off Frost and picked a branch from the ground to lean on like a crutch. I've never seen him do this before. "Are all those fields yours?" He swings the branch across the horizon, pointing—oh. That's going to get annoying.

"Right down to the river. I thought Demetrios here might escort you while I settle your family. He knows far more than I do about it all, isn't that right, Demetrios? He's been steward since I was a baby."

The old man bares his gums again in his infant's grin.

"Nico!" Euphranor has taken to barking at my little brother like a soldier, which has him giddy. He gets down from the pony and stands at attention, pale and peaky and as serious as possible, probably hoping to be asked to extinguish a forest fire or bear some great weight. Clever Euphranor slings a waterskin over his shoulder and hands him a bow and arrows. "Perhaps a bit of hunting, later, when your mother's not paying attention," he stage-whispers.

Myrmex has to come over to us; has to. Hunting! He can't be left out. He stands closer to me than usual, waiting for his assignment.

"Come, ladies." Euphranor takes a few steps. Perhaps he senses Myrmex's face hardening, because he looks back and slaps himself on the forehead. "Pinch, good man! Get that basket, would you?"

Myrmex nods at Pyrrhaios, who hefts the picnic basket and follows us at a distance. Daddy and the old man are already deep in conversation, and Daddy doesn't even notice us leave. He has that cock-headed, flare-nostrilled attention that says everyone around him is to be silent so he can learn.

❧

We picnic in a pine grove on a horse blanket thrown over a carpet of sappy needles. Piny wine and thick, slow sunshine I can taste. "Eat your bread," Herpyllis says, but I'm not hungry. Wine and sunlight, sunlight and shade and wine. I take my cup down the slope to look at the pond, all overhung with goldenrod and forsythia. The surface of the water is thick and still and spackled with golden pollen, Demetrios's scum.

Something leaps behind me; I feel the air move.

My brother, naked; he lands in the pond with an almighty air-spangling splash, and comes up coated in gold. He floats on his back for a moment to give me a look at everything, then arches lazily and goes down smooth as a dolphin: throat, chest, softness, thighs, knees, feet, toes. The pollen has fled from the centre of the pond to limn the banks yellow, leaving a cool black hole. He surfaces again, smiles; wants me to come in. A little less golden, now, after the second dip. I feel the honey letting down between my legs. I shake my head.

"You see," Euphranor says behind me, softly. He hasn't stepped from the shadows, knows Myrmex doesn't know he's there. "That's all it needed. Cleared nicely now. Shall we go in?"

*The three of us.* Doors and the windows all opening. *Oh!*

"Next time."

Euphranor smiles, catching my veil as I pass him on my way back up the hill, and trails its full white length through his fingertips before he lets it go.

Shouting from the distance. Nico and Herpyllis, on the blanket, look up from their perusal of the sweets. They look at me; I shrug. Then we can make it out: Demetrios calling his master. "He's at the pond," I tell Herpyllis. "I just left him there. I'll get him."

Back down the slope, the ghost of my veil reeling me back down and in. But there's only Myrmex, supine in the golden-rod, who starts when he sees me and covers himself with his hands. The gold is gone, and instead he's pink all over from the exertion of what he's just been doing.

"You haven't seen Euphranor?"

He shudders, sighs.

Back up the slope again, where I find Euphranor listening to a puffing Demetrios, while Nico struggles to ready the horses.

"Your father is injured," Euphranor says curtly. "Where are the others?"

"Mummy went looking for mushrooms," Nico stammers. "Pyrrhaios went with her. I don't know where Myrmex is."

"Injured how?" I look from Euphranor to Demetrios. Neither is smiling.

Demetrios glances at his master, who nods. "Twist of the ankle, Lady," he says. "Already puffed up like a melon. He can't walk on it, but I reckon he'll live."

I'm moving.

"Child, wait." Euphranor hurries to catch up to me. "Do you ride? It might be faster if I were to lead you on your brother's little—"

I start to jog.

Back at the house, Daddy is sitting on a cart as though we've kept him waiting a long time. I hear Demetrios telling his master he left him inside, on a couch.

"What happened?" I climb up beside him to look.

He grunts and lifts his hem. His left ankle is a purple ball. I smell the vomit, though his face and clothes are clean. A lot of pain, then.

"Why do you sit this way?" I whisper. "You're the one who taught me—"

He lets me help him to lying, my hand supporting his heavy head. He lets me lift the good foot onto the bench, and then the bad. White with the pain, now. I scooch one of the silly purple silk cushions under the ankle to elevate it, and tell Nico to get a cold cloth. "Long enough for binding," I tell him. He nods and disappears into the house, ignoring Euphranor. Now who's the soldier?

Daddy is talking about which plant to use for the

compress. "At home," I tell him. "Right now, let's just get home."

He retches once while Nico holds the foot up and I bind his ankle. Euphranor sends Demetrios to look for the others. Myrmex appears and himself wipes Daddy's mouth with a clean damp cloth. Euphranor draws Myrmex aside and says something to him in an undertone I can't hear. I hear Myrmex tell him Daddy needs to be kept warm. They're both frowning, serious, co-operating. Euphranor touches Myrmex's shoulder and points into the house. Myrmex goes inside and comes out a moment later with a fur he tucks around Daddy, against shock. He knows without being told, like Nico and me. More than Demetrios. More than Euphranor.

Herpyllis and Pyrrhaios appear, breathless, leading the horses.

"Where have you been?" Daddy asks, looking up at her, his love. She sits beside him the whole journey home, holding his hand, gazing into his face. There's dirt on her dress and a twig in her hair. When I draw the twig out, she opens the pouch on her hip to show me her dozen creamy, dirty finds.

We will have eggs with mushrooms for supper.

"What about Daddy's farm?" Nico asks in a small voice, and Euphranor promises he'll take us another day, when Daddy's better.

"Agrimony," I tell Daddy. The plant he was trying to remember. "I'll make you an agrimony poultice for the swelling. Try not to move so much."

Daddy, pushing the fur down, says he's hot.

"No, Myrmex is right," I say. "Better hot than cold."

The rest of the ride home we are silent, chastened. I try to remember what we might have left behind at the picnic site, the pond, the field. Food, wine, the blanket, my veil. A small spoonful of Myrmex's pleasure. Herpyllis's virtue.

My sandals, abandoned in the field so I could run.

✺

Agrimony, what Herpyllis calls cocklebur, grows like a weed along the roadside. I wrap my hands in leather to pluck the leaves, and pile some burs in the courtyard for Nico, who uses them for darts. Cooked with bran and vinegar, the leaves makes a sticky, stinky mess that Daddy soon tires of.

"Lie still," I order. He groans and squirms while I try to wrap a cloth around his pasted ankle, getting smears everywhere, until finally he demands the pot like a sulky child who suddenly can't wait any longer. So now he must stand, and I mustn't watch. I put my hands over my eyes and listen to his effortful dribble, and help him back to lying once he's dropped his clothes back over himself, smearing the poultice even further. As the days go by he complains of headaches, too, and insomnia, and whines if we leave him alone for too long. He makes Myrmex read to him, and—when Myrmex is too slow—me. Herpyllis tries sitting with us, once or twice, but she bores quickly, and Daddy complains when she starts pottering around the room, dusting or straightening the sheets or picking over the flowers she cut for him the night we got home, pinching off the dead bits. She's nervous lately, quick to tears, and when Daddy starts talking about the dead king, she bites her fist and leaves the room.

More and more he talks about the king. His grief now—clouded by the pain in his ankle, maybe—is tinctured by bitterness, until you'd think they never loved each other at all. He rants. Alexander wouldn't listen, wouldn't learn, not so bright after all, just a vicious little boy. Never a man, not really. In the body, but never in the mind.

I am not thinking of Myrmex.

Daddy wrote him letters, hundreds of letters. The army was under orders from no less than Antipater himself to have them included in dispatches, but never once a reply. That's not love, Daddy says. All that he gave him, and never once a word back.

"But he sent all those specimens," I remind him. "Fish skeletons, fossilized birds, dried flowers. To you, no one else. So something reached him."

"I don't doubt my letters reached him," Daddy says stiffly. "As I have just said."

"Not your letters." I hold a cup to his lips for him to sip. Utterly unnecessary, but he's malingering now, a week later, and demands these little services. "Your—thoughts. Your love of him. Those things reached him, and he reached back to you."

"You're a sweet girl," Daddy says.

The next day there's a gleam in his eye I recognize, and fear. With much production, he has himself carried to his study and set up on cushions, with drink and nibbles and books and pen and paper ready to hand. He insists Ambracis sit beside him in case he should need her to fetch anything, leaving all the kitchen work to Thale, who slams the pots just enough to let us know how much she resents the younger woman's easy day. Ambracis, in turn, may not move or rustle or swallow too loudly in case she should throw off Daddy's train of thought; nor may she respond when the baby calls for her. I pass by once or twice and see her sitting miserably while it screams from where Thale has tethered it to the table in the kitchen so she can keep an eye on it and do her chores too. It quiets when Olympios stops by, but he has work to do. I try to play with it myself a bit, but it knows the difference, and is fretful all the day.

"What's he doing?" I ask Herpyllis, but she doesn't know.

By evening he's ready to show us: drawings. Designs, actually, for statues of his dead: of his parents; his brother, Uncle Proxenus, and Proxenus's wife; Daddy's little sister, who died in childbirth when her son, my cousin Nicanor, was a tot. He's with the army now, Nicanor, in the East. We assume he's alive.

"I will have them erected in Stageira," Daddy announces. "The village of my birth. And, in thanks for Nicanor's return, I propose statues of Zeus and Athena also, life-size."

Now I know he is mad.

"Is Nicanor returned?" I say carefully.

Daddy ignores me, carefully rolling his drawings.

"How big *are* Zeus and Athena?" I ask. "In life?"

"Go to your room," Daddy says.

The drawings are tentative, in Daddy's quavering old-man's hand. He intends to commission a famous sculptor, an Athenian named Gryllion, to execute them. He'll send Tycho to deliver the commission. For the next three days, he works and works on his awful drawings, and speaks of nothing else. On the fourth day, Ambracis whispers he is bedridden, and refuses to eat.

I nod, and she shakes her head. We know the pattern.

Two weeks after the injury, after three days in his room, he summons me to his bedside. He's sitting up, supported by many pillows. His ankle is much less swollen, though he still affects to close his eyes and quiver when I touch it with gentlest fingertips.

"Daughter," he says. "Leave that. I have brought you here today to discuss your future."

*Brought me here*—as though I haven't been in and out of the room every hour, seeing to his needs while the blackness grips him. Spooning in the broth, steadying the bedpan, flapping the curtain to freshen the air. Combing his hair.

"Piffle," I say.

"You shall marry cousin Nicanor," Daddy says. "Just as soon as he returns from Persia."

A moment of utter smoothness, pure emptiness, before thinking resumes.

"I'm—you—because of—what?" I say.

"Pardon?" Daddy says.

"Pardon?"

"That's better," Daddy says. "You shall marry Nicanor. You remember Nicanor."

"Why?" I say.

"Do you remember Nicanor?"

So he has scripted this, and I must play my part. "I remember him from when I was a baby. I haven't seen him in—twelve summers?"

"What do you remember?"

*Running. Trees. Arms around my waist, lifting me to reach a plum.*
*Don't eat it. Give it to Mummy. Come on, Pytho. One for you and one for*
*me. Come on. Hold my hand. Where's your plum?*

"Nothing," I say.

"Don't be angry," Daddy says. "I had to."

He shows me the document he's written: his will.

"How many summers is he?"

"Forty-four," Daddy says.

A sound like laughter comes out of me. "No."

Daddy frowns. "Why not?"

"Why?"

He gestures at himself, the bed.

"There's nothing wrong with you," I say.

He looks at his lap.

"How do you even know he's alive?"

"I'm making enquiries."

I shake my head. "I won't."

"Who, then?"

I open my mouth but nothing comes.

"He's a good man," Daddy says. "I remember him very well.
A serious, intelligent, kind man. Kin."

I think he's probably dead. I think Daddy will make his
enquiries and he will find out Nicanor is dead and then we'll
think about who else is kin. That's what I think. I can keep
quiet until then.

"Good girl," Daddy says, when I say nothing.

He talks me through the rest of the will. For comic relief,
he proposes Theophrastos as an alternative should Nicanor be
unable or unwilling. (*Or dead, since he will be dead.*) I contain

myself admirably and he notices nothing. He walks me through the slaves, the properties, Nico. Nico will stay with me, that's one thing. I tell him I like that.

"You see," he says, looking up, squeezing my hand.

Myrmex, he says, will be sent back to his own people. I say nothing.

Herpyllis, now.

But here he stops; his face works in pain. I hold his hand until he can talk again.

"She has been good to me," he says. "After your mother—"

He looks at his lap, shakes his head. One tear falls. Two. Two blots on the sheet. He looks back up at me. Straight at me, clear-eyed, and I see the script is gone. "You can live without love," he says. "You think you can't, at your age. I was your age, once, too."

"How do you do that?" I ask.

"You care," he says slowly. "You take care. You care for the body and the mind, you behave kindly, you are generous. You put her needs before your own. Sweet food, fresh air, clean clothes, safety. You offer these things. You offer the warmth of yourself. As to a baby. For me, it helped to think of her as a baby, or a little girl. You can offer so much affection and care, who would know the difference?"

"Is that what you did?"

He touches my cheek. "Not always as well as I could have. But if I could do it all again, I would do it that way."

"Do you not—" I begin, but can't finish the sentence.

"Love you?" Daddy says. "Did you think I was talking about you? Little Pythias. Did you think I was talking about you?"

When we are both back inside ourselves again, he tells me what he's planned for Herpyllis. He is generous: choice of properties, money, furniture, everything she might want.

"There is one more thing," Daddy says. "I want her to marry. I want her to have that, if she wants it. I want to give her what she needs, in memory of all my gratitude towards her. If she wants it."

"I think she might," I say.

"I think I'll give her Pyrrhaios, also," Daddy says. "She's used to living with servants."

Without looking at him to see what he does or doesn't know, is or isn't saying, I agree that's a fine idea.

"We shall all be brave," Daddy says. "The worst never lasts long. Especially if you've thought through all the alternatives, and you have a plan."

And that, when you think about it, is a very fine idea indeed.

✺

In my room—twilight, curtains drawn—the brazier sends up a single thread of acrid smoke, the stink of burning hair. I do it in whispers.

> *Bring to perfection this binding spell in order that he may never have experience of another than me alone, Pythias, daughter of Aristotle; that he be enslaved, driven mad, fly through the air in search of me, that he bring his thigh to my thigh and his nature to my nature, always and for the rest of his life. Drag him by the hair and the guts to me. Burn, torch his soul, his*

*body, his limbs. Lay him low with fever, unceasing sickness, incomprehensible sickness, until he comes to me. Take away his sleep until he comes to please my soul. Lead him, loving, burning on account of his love and desire for me, Pythias, daughter of Aristotle. Impel, force him to come to me, to love me, to give me what I want. Now, now, quickly, quickly.*

"Are you insane?"

Herpyllis stands with her hands on her hips while Daddy, happy as a dog, whaps his head vigorously to one side, trying to drain the water from his ear. His cheeks are a rude pink and his hair is still damp.

"Not at all!" he shouts, swim-deafened. "We're going again tomorrow."

When he's limped off to look for a towel, Herpyllis rounds on me. "You'll kill him."

I wring the cloth he wrapped around his parts into the plants.

"Idiot!" Herpyllis snatches it from me. "That's salt water. You'll kill my herbs. Where did you take him, anyway?"

"The beach just north of the channel. He can walk when he wants to, you know, so long as he has his stick. It's not that far."

"Swimming." Herpyllis spits onto the ground. "Give this to Ambracis. She can take it to the river when she goes with the other laundry. In the sea, in his condition."

"He gets exercise that way with no pressure on the ankle." I take the wet wad back from her. "You saw his face. It cheers him up like you wouldn't—"

"You'll kill him." Grumbling now, though, instead of angry. "Well, that'll be on your head. Does he even remember how to swim?"

I'd sat on a rock while he undressed. His skin was so pale, age-freckled, and he had soft flab in places I'd never seen. Still, it was as though the ghost of a younger man inspirited his body, guided his movements; he had the unconscious confidence of actions he'd been performing for six decades. He'd said nothing to me during the walk, a walk he didn't resist; he was too far gone. I held his arm, and he leaned heavily on me. I could smell the old-man smell of him, the must, and hear the effort of his breathing. At the beach I simply told him to undress, and he did. I told him to go in. He looked at me, then dropped his stick and limped into the surf. At knee-depth he put his hands over his head and dived. It took him a long time to come up. I made the decision not to go in after him. Instead, I dug at the sand with my toes, working my feet in and in and in until I found wet.

"Pytho!"

A long way out, one arm in the air. Holding something up. I walked down to the shore, lifting up my skirts, and he swam in to meet me and hand me his find: an anemone. Immediately he turned back, and dived down again.

I gave the anemone to Tycho and lay back on the rock, eyes closed.

"He remembers," I say to Herpyllis.

That night he calls me to his study and we dissect his specimens. He lets me slit the underbelly of an orange starfish he kept damp, and therefore alive, so I can see the contraction of the muscles, the death-wince. He shows me the anemone's mouth, a star-shaped, petalled orifice, and explains its digestion. He shucks a clam and sets me the exercise of describing it, both in words and drawings. When I bid him goodnight and gather the papers up to take to my room, he asks if he might keep them with his own notes. I go to sleep thinking about my drawings on his desk. This is the first time he's asked to keep any work of mine.

We start going to the beach every afternoon. Nico whines when we try to get him to come; he's befriended a local boy and they're off together most days, whooping through the trees with the puppy and annoying the neighbours. Herpyllis too refuses to come, though not angrily; she stands in the doorway, waving fondly, and is there to greet us with a big dry towel when we return. She bustles busily around us, ignoring the servants. Pyrrhaios is nowhere to be seen. Well. Mentally I superimpose my drawings of our specimens—the labial moistness of the clam, the petalled orifice of the anemone's throat, the spasms of the dying starfish—on Herpyllis's hole.

Daddy, basking in his new mobility, swims a little longer each day even as the weather cools. Fall is coming, singeing the trees red and prettying Daddy, who rises from the waves all steaming in the cold, holding the cloth around his parts with one hand and clutching shellfish to his breast with the other, my very own Aphrodite of the Specimens. His eyes are clearer, and he smiles sometimes. Occasionally he makes a little joke. He has a permanent limp now, but no longer complains of it; it's become a part of him. Once I watched him wade through the shallows, looking for limpets, quietly singing. Each day

I ask him how he's feeling. "Quiet," he'll say, or "Steady." Once, a day like any other, he told me he thought he felt joy.

"You think?" I said.

He shrugged. After a moment's carefully considered silence, we looked at each other and laughed.

That evening, after supper, he says he wants to swim the channel where it's narrowest. "The soldiers do it just as the tide's turning," he says. "I've watched them. Pushed one way by the current, then the other. Good fun."

"Nonsense," Herpyllis says.

"Fun *and* science," Daddy says. "It's a unique phenomenon. Awfully famous."

"You're already awfully famous," Herpyllis says. "What on earth are you going to learn from being pushed around in the current like a fig in a custard?"

"Ah," Daddy says. "But you see, I intend to dive. To observe the behaviour of the marine life during the phenomenon. I shall gather—"

"—specimens—" Nico, Herpyllis and I say with one voice.

"—and study them," Daddy says serenely. "For my book."

Herpyllis rolls her eyes. Nico runs off to find the puppy.

"A new one?" I ask.

"A collaboration," Daddy says.

I can't imagine who with; Theophrastos is still in Athens. Then he smiles and I blush.

"You'll come watch me, won't you, pet?" he asks. "Hold my towel? Cheer me on?"

Tycho's a shadow in the doorway.

"Can Tycho come, too?" I ask.

Daddy nods. Tycho disappears.

"You like him," Daddy says. "You trust him. I think I'll amend my will and give him to you, when you get married."

I say, "Ah."

"You remind me," Daddy says. "I'll do it after my swim. Let's go check the charts for the tide."

It turns out the optimal time is dawn. "Seriously?" I say, thinking of my warm bed. "Couldn't we just wait twelve hours?"

"It'll be dark by then," Daddy says.

"Dawn's pretty dark, too."

"Lazy pet. You'll survive one early morning. Have you ever seen the colour of the sky that early in the day? The sun comes up like fine wine."

I pretend to shudder and he smiles that rare, sweet smile.

I'm woken by the tap of his fingers on my door jamb, while the sky is still black and the cock is still sleeping. I tie my hair back uncombed into a pony's tail, and put on my warmest clothes. It's really cold; hoarfrost on the grass.

Once we're away from the houses and our voices won't disturb anyone, I exhale hard, like Nico trying to offend me with his garlic breath, to make a white plume in the air. "There must be fire in us," I say to Daddy. "Or something like embers. In the heart, maybe? To make smoke like this?"

Daddy says nothing.

At the narrowest part of the channel, we pick our way down the rocky slopes to the water. Daddy starts to undress.

"Ho!" calls a man passing on the near bank with a horse and cart.

"Good morning!" Daddy calls back, undressing.

"Is he sick?" the man calls to me.

I shake my head.

"Look, he's got milk," Daddy says. "Take some coins from my bag, there, and my cup, and get some for after my swim. It's early enough; it's probably still warm."

"I'll do it," I tell Tycho. *Stay with him.*

I pick my way up the slope, holding my skirts up, while the man waits, staring at Daddy. When I hold out the coin, he asks me again if Daddy is sick. I shake my head.

"Then he's an idiot." The man fills Daddy's cup with milk, which steams in the cold. I realize how stupid my idea was. Embers in the heart, seriously. That's why Daddy didn't reply. "The current's about to change. You're not from here, are you?"

"He knows about the current."

"He doesn't know anything." There's a splash and the man cries out. Daddy's in. The man says an evil word. He reaches under his seat for a length of rope and jumps down awkwardly from his cart. He hands me the horse's reins and tells me not to let go. He scrabbles down the bank, tripping once, but doesn't stop to inspect the scrape to his knee which, even from here, I can see is bleeding. Daddy is mid-channel now, treading water in what seems to be a lull. The man coils the rope, then tosses the end to Daddy. Confused, Daddy reaches for the end, but it drifts out of his reach. Now Daddy is moving, but not swimming. He dives.

The man asks Tycho what the evil word Daddy thinks he's

doing, and did Tycho and I come down here to help him kill himself, and if so we're evil words ourselves. I feel his anger on me like spit. Beside me, the horse shifts and snuffles nervously. It pulls its head against the reins, testing me, smelling inexperience. Smelling girl.

People on both banks have stopped to watch now, adults and children with early-morning business. The sky has indeed gone tender, pink and frail and fine. A shout goes up from the onlookers: Daddy has surfaced, considerably north of where he went in. He's trying to swim back to us, but the current is holding him prisoner, and he's swimming hard just to stay still. People are shouting and waving their arms, *That way, that way,* wanting him to swim with the current rather than against it. He dives again.

The crowd makes a soft, hurt sound, fist to the gut.

I scan the crowd for someone I recognize: one of the men from Plios's party, a soldier, Euphranor himself? But it's too early in the morning for the quality, and all I see are slaves, market-women, vagrants. Each face shows horror.

The milkman is beside me. "Come on," he says. "He'll wash up on the beach there." He points towards our swimming beach. "If he washes up."

I climb up onto the cart beside him and he *tchas* the horse into a trot. At the head of the beach path, he ties the reins to a stump. Tycho and I run on ahead.

The beach is empty.

"No," the man says, puffing up behind me. "No, no, no," like he's forbidding me something. My arm shoots out to point to something far out in the bay: a head. The man strips angrily to pudge-buttocked bareness and wades in, then dives. Tycho is ahead of him. Tycho swims out to Daddy and brings him back, expertly, in a kind of swimming headlock. When they're fifty paces out, I wade in myself, waist-deep, to help bring him the rest of the way. Daddy's face is white and his eyes are closed.

On the sand, Tycho wraps his own clothes around Daddy and rubs him hard all over his body. The onlookers have caught up with us now, and someone has a blanket for the milkman. I rub Daddy the way Tycho does, sitting beside him on the sand, propping him up against my body. Tycho is blue-lipped and shivering convulsively now.

Someone dumps a blanket over Tycho's shoulders, and another over my legs. Perhaps I'm crying.

"Pythias," Daddy says quietly, without opening his eyes.

The crowd exhales. The air goes white from the ember in every chest.

✸◉✸

At home, Herpyllis proves she could have made a soldier. She has Daddy put to bed wrapped in sheets warmed with stones heated in the fire; gives the milkman a set of new clothes, a hot meal and a bag of coins; thanks Tycho; and slaps me across the face.

She spends the rest of the day at Daddy's bedside, spooning hot broth into his mouth and singing to him like she does to Nico when he gets a tummy ache. I can hear her soft voice from my bedroom, which she's ordered me not to leave.

Daddy soon gets a cold. He snots and sneezes and aches all

over, he says, and where is Pythias? Herpyllis relents, and lets me in to see him.

"Hello, pet," he says.

I ask him how he's feeling. Herpyllis snorts.

"Fine, fine," he says, and then he coughs until his face goes purple. He waves angrily at Herpyllis to leave the room.

"It's nothing," he says, when the coughing stops. "She's hysterical."

"She's not."

He pats the bedside and I sit. "She loves us both," he says. "She knows you were trying to help."

I hold his hand for a while, his baby-soft hand.

"A child is a line cast blind to the future," he says. "Like an idea, or a book. Who knows where it will land, or what it will draw out?"

I ask him if he'd like me to write that down.

"No, pet," he says. "That's just for you."

I think we're both joking.

※◎※

The cough stays with him. He begins to cough up a yellowish thickness that Herpyllis says is a good sign; it's the sickness coming out. He runs a low fever and has shivering fits. He eats little and drenches the sheets with night sweats. Still, he gets up sometimes, to use the pot or sit for short periods in the garden in the thin autumn sun. He asks for books, not to read, but just to hold on his lap. Sometimes I read to him. When he coughs, now, he holds a hand to his chest against the pain. His lips are permanently blue. Moving from bed to chair is enough to make him gasp like a runner at the end of a race. He takes to coughing into a cloth. Herpyllis does this laundry, angrily forbidding me or the servants to help. She thinks she can carry this secret by herself.

After a week of coughing blood, he lies down to die. It takes four more days. He complains of stabbing pains in his side, and his skin takes on a blue tinge all over.

"What did you see?" I ask him, late one night. I'm sitting with him so Herpyllis can sleep a bit. "What did you see down there, Daddy?"

His shallow breaths rasp like a saw.

When the cock crows, I go to wake Herpyllis. She takes one look at Daddy and sends me to get Nico, and Myrmex and everyone. The slaves, everyone. *Now, now, quickly, quickly.*

He's still breathing when we get back.

❧❀❧

Herpyllis herself lays the coin on his tongue, and together we bathe him and dew him with sweet oil. We dress him warmly in white for his journey, and when Thale returns from the meadow with a basket of fall flowers we weave a tiny wildflower garland for his lovely head: creamy fall anemones, purple crocuses, white winter violets, pink cyclamen. Herpyllis puts the honey cake for the dog in his hand and holds his fingers closed over it until they stiffen. We wear our darkest clothes to contrast Daddy, to show we are still with the living, and the pain of that.

The next day is the laying-out. Pyrrhaios and Tycho carry the bed to the front hall and point his feet to the door. Herpyllis, Nico, Myrmex and I sit around him, fanning away the flies. To Thale falls the coming and going: fetching white jars from the market for perfumes to keep the body bearable, sweeping up the dried marjoram and strewing fresh on the floor, trying to get the four of us to drink and Nico to take a bit of bread. Herpyllis rips her hair from its pins and lets it hang; I pull mine out, slowly, strand by strand, until Herpyllis takes my hands in hers and says enough. *Enough*; though she comes back from a visit to the pot with bloody claw-marks on both cheeks and on the tops of her breasts. When she forbids me to do the same, I know she's worried about scarring before my marriage. I touch my fingertips to her blood, instead, and swipe it onto my face, where it mixes with the tears and eventually dries. We are quiet, against tradition—no keening—but we know it's what Daddy would want.

On the third day is the procession. Herpyllis has left the body only to use the pot and put Nico to bed. Herpyllis and Myrmex and I dozed sitting up with him and are weak with hunger and exhaustion now. We set out before sunrise. Pyrrhaios, Simon, Tycho and Myrmex carry the bed. Behind them walk the singers Thale found, sisters from Caria who know the old mourning songs. Professionals: their voices are thin and bird-like, their eyes blank. Nico and I come last, holding hands; Herpyllis—no marriage, no tie of blood—stands in the doorway, watching us go.

We walk away from the sunrise, to the road into town, to the markers we passed when we first arrived. The gravesman is waiting by a hole in the ground. Nico steps forward to help lift Daddy into the clay coffin. "On his side," the gravesman says. The only thing he says. They lay Daddy on his side like a sleeping child so that when he's lowered into the ground he'll face west. We take turns approaching him. Myrmex places the three white perfume jars at Daddy's head and hands and feet. I put a book of seashell sketches inside his clothes, against his breast, because his arms and hands are too stiff now to manoeuvre into an embrace, and at any rate he's still holding the dried-up cake. Nico is last. He has the lamp Herpyllis gave him, and a tablet and stylus of his own. I notice he glances up at Pyrrhaios as he's placing them by Daddy's hands and Pyrrhaios nods, *That's right*.

The gravesman closes the coffin and the men lower it, suspended on ropes, into the hole. They shovel the dirt over and erect the marble stone. Thale hands me the basket of olives, honey and wildflowers, which I place on the grave. Myrmex pours a cup of milk over the raw earth, and it's done.

When we get home—all but Myrmex, who peeled away from us into town—Herpyllis is holding a letter that came by courier while we were at the grave. Theophrastos will host the funeral feast for Daddy's colleagues and students—*those who were closest to him*, he writes—in Athens.

Daddy is travelling. The coin will be gone by now, and the cake. He's on his way.

※◎※

We sit in the public room in the home of Thaulos, a high-ceilinged reception room with severe furniture and only a single small brazier in one corner. Herpyllis is in the middle of a couch with Nico on one side and me on the other, a wing around each of us. My hair is cropped short, like a boy's; Nico's will be allowed to grow shaggy.

"The children have been ill," she says, when neither of us answers his greeting.

She still wears her darkest dress, sweat-smelling after so many days without washing, and no make-up; her eyes are a mess. Nico drones softly to himself, a wordless keening. He's been doing this for days. I find it important not to speak. Each word feels precious, suddenly, and so many words are so utterly unnecessary.

"Your father named Antipater as executor of his will," Thaulos begins. Antipater, regent of Macedon, my father's old friend. "I stand here today as his proxy."

"I thank you," Herpyllis says.

Thaulos takes a breath to speak, then changes his mind. He rubs his forehead, reading over the paper in front of him. Finally he looks up. "It's a pickle, isn't it?" he says kindly.

We can only breathe.

"I've sent word to your father's school in Athens, to"—he squints at the paper—"Theophrastos, and to the nephew, in dispatches. His unit is still in Babylon. Nicanor, yes? Your intended?" He's looking at me.

"He's dead," I say.

"Shh." Herpyllis kisses my hair.

"Nicanor is dead."

Thaulos looks surprised.

"He's dead," I say again.

"Then you have better intelligence than I do." He smiles gently at his own joke. "I've received no such report. The army prides itself on accuracy in such matters. I wish I'd known you had such worries. I could have eased your mind."

"Is he coming home?" Herpyllis asks.

Now Thaulos frowns.

"They've been coming home ever since they left," I say. "Years ago. That's what Daddy always said. All we can do is wait."

"Your father had a unique insight into the mind of our king," Thaulos says. "I think his great wisdom guides us even now."

"She has the spark of him in her," Herpyllis says. "She always did."

I go blank for a few seconds, and when I come back they're discussing Herpyllis's future.

"Of course," she's saying, bowing her head obediently. "Of course."

"You have people there still?"

"A sister," Herpyllis says. "Cousins."

"And the boy will go to Theophrastos."

"Myrmex, you mean." Herpyllis nods.

Thaulos looks at the papers again.

"Mummy?" Nico says.

"*Nicanor shall take charge of the boy Myrmex, that he be taken to his own friends in a manner worthy of me with the property of his which we received*," Thaulos reads. "Orphan, is he? No, I mean the other boy. This fine fellow here. Would you like to go to school? Nicomachos, is it? I'm sure it's what your father would have wanted for you."

Nico screams, a high thin sound like a hawk. Herpyllis

lets go of me to put both her arms around him. Her shoulders are shaking.

Thaulos, obviously startled, stands. I stand too, while Herpyllis and Nico hold each other, weeping. With a look, he bids me follow him over to the window, where they won't hear us. We look out on a drill team going through manoeuvres. "And you?" he says.

I wait.

"You can go to Athens with your brother." Watching his soldiers, Thaulos stands taller with unconscious pride. "I'm familiar with your father's concerns, but I can reassure you that they were—overstated, shall we say. Macedon controls Athens. You will be safe there."

I thank him.

"I suppose you could go with the woman, alternatively," he muses. "Like a mother to you, is she? A girl needs a mother. You could wait with her in Stageira for your intended. Confidentially, I suspect the army will move quickly now to return home. Now that the king's ambitions are no longer—"

"Now that there is no longer a god to lead them," I say.

Thaulos looks at his feet.

"How long?" I ask.

"Months. A year at most, I'd guess, for all of them to return. Think about it. I have a daughter myself, though younger than you. I understand there are preparations for a marriage? Certain information to be passed on? Household management and so on? And then learning how to care for all the little ones to come?"

I think he is a kind daddy.

"I'll leave your decision to the wisdom you've inherited from your father." He gives me the paper and holds a hand toward the door, conducting us out. Nico is quiet now, and he and Herpyllis have both risen. Our interview is done. "He will guide you."

"Always," I say.

Outside, Pyrrhaios leans down to murmur something in Nico's ear. Nico stands a little straighter, wiping his face, and Pyrrhaios briefly puts a hand on his shoulder. He must have heard everything. Herpyllis walks slowly, already trying to delay the inevitable.

At home, I find Myrmex and give him the paper. He reads it slowly, then once more, even more slowly. I realize he's drunk.

"'Taken to his own friends in a manner worthy of me with the property of his which we received.'" Myrmex spits at my feet. "What property? What friends?"

"I don't know," I whisper.

He reads a third time. "There was a bag," he says slowly. "They gave me a bag to give to your father, when I left home, when I came to Athens. It was sewn closed. I bet it was money. My money."

I want to kiss him.

"Your brother'll give it to me, if you won't."

"I've been in the storeroom," I say, stupidly. "I've never seen such a bag." I stand up so he can press himself against me if he wants to.

"Tight as your father," he sneers. And off he goes to rant at poor terrified Nico, until Herpyllis flaps him away like she flaps the chickens with her skirts.

"I'll get what's mine," Myrmex says. "I'll find a way."

He clangs out of the front gate, leaving it bouncing behind him.

Herpyllis begins packing. Nico sits in a corner, his gaze following her everywhere. Sometimes he rocks a little. Herpyllis's eyes are now so raw and swollen I fear infection. She lets me examine her. I make her cold compresses with bruised mint, but, privately, I fear whatever prettiness she might once have had is gone forever.

The next morning, Myrmex still isn't back.

"He needs to grieve," Herpyllis says. "Not everyone can share grief." She puts aside what she's been doing, some last mending for Nico, and pats the couch beside her. "I've been wanting to speak to you, Pytho."

I sit.

"What I said when you took him swimming that first time," she begins. "About how it would be on your head."

I shake my head to show I know she didn't mean it that way.

"No, you listen," she says. "You're going to let me say it aloud. You didn't do this. You didn't make it, you didn't wish it, you didn't cause it in any way. You were not the cause. Neither material, formal, efficient, nor final."

I look at her.

"That was a joke," she says.

We embrace for a long time while Nico watches us silently from his corner. When Herpyllis finally releases me and I stand, he comes to take my place. I sit back down, and she and I hold him from both sides.

Herpyllis leaves for Stageira the next morning, with Pyrrhaios and everything else accorded her in the will. Some very nice furniture. While she and Nico hug fiercely, I give them the gift I've been saving to make their parting possible.

"You'll both come to my wedding," I say. "It'll only be a few months to wait, and then you'll be together again."

Herpyllis embraces me, and it's only then I realize—stupidly—she's actually leaving me, too. "Who loves you?" she whispers into my hair.

*You do.*

"There, that's not so bad, is it?" she says to Nico. He sniffles a smile. She kisses my cheek, crushes him to her one last time, and mounts the waiting cart. "Kiss Myrmex for me," she calls.

Nico pulls me inside to find Daddy's map of the East, to figure out exactly where his mother is going and how long until Nicanor might make it home from the wars. I play along, gravely calculating, trying to factor in rivers and seasons.

We eat a quiet supper together in the innermost court-yard, the one with the lavender. Nico will leave for Athens and Theophrastos in the morning; Thaulos has offered to convey him with some troops who are shifting there. He'll be most utterly safe at school—Theophrastos loves him like a dog loves a ball. I tell him I'll be back in Athens myself very soon, once everything in Daddy's will is wrapped up here. There are matters to be seen to, bills to be paid, loose ends to be tied.

"Where's Myrmex?" Nico asks.

"I don't know."

Nico looks at me with his big, dark, clear eyes.

We go together to the storeroom and consider the iron bars holding the door.

"Nico, he wouldn't," I say. "He'd had too much to drink, that's all. Everyone grieves differently."

"Who's got the key?" Nico says.

Thale, it turns out; Herpyllis gave it to her before she left, telling her to give it to me when I was ready.

The door swings open easily, silently; recent oiling. Bags of corn and beans and lentils and flour; seeds, dried herbs, squash; the first apples of the year. Wine, lamp oil, cooking oil, torches, wool.

"Lady," Thale whispers.

Every last coin is gone.

❦

Who am I to be making decisions? Who am I? An orphan, a pauper. A girl. Thinking thinking thinking smiling smiling smiling. Grace matters now.

"But how did he get in?" Nico says.

"Before Herpyllis left, probably. Sometimes she left the key lying around in the kitchen, on market days when she was in and out of there a lot."

"It's not her fault."

"Of course not." I reassure Nico, reassure the servants. "Silly boy," I say, over and over, meaning Myrmex. "He'll be back."

"Lady," they say. I read their doubts, but they'll take the lead from me. There's no one else. Late at night, I count the coins I keep in my own little purse, with my clothes in the trunk in my room. I can afford a week; two, at most.

Of course I forgive him.

Once the stars are up and the house is quiet, I go to wake Tycho, who sleeps by the front gate. "Come," I say.

We walk down to the beach. I expected some objection—he's been with us so long, Tycho, that occasionally he'll risk some such—but he says nothing. Standing on the sand, we both stare into the black water.

"I should have followed him in," Tycho says. "Lady, forgive me."

I walk straight down to the water's edge, then keep walking.

The water is cold and then colder; the plunge stops my heart. I surface gasping and look back. Tycho is watching me.

I dive again, eyes open. There's a faint phosphorescence in the water that licks me greeny-gold. I sob under the surface, come up to breathe, go down again to let more tears go. I'm almost done when I hear Tycho's deep call.

"Almost," I call back. "Almost."

I chose night on purpose; no one to see me, no one to shock. Girls don't swim. But when I wade up onto the sand, my dress plastered to me, cold past feeling, I see a light back in the trees.

"Quickly," Tycho says, wrapping his wool around me. He's seen it, too.

Movement through the trees; someone walking.

We come out onto the road in silence, my wet feet chafing in my sandals. I know Tycho wants to throw me over his shoulder and carry me, like he used to when I was little. Whoever's got the lamp cut through the trees to come out ahead of us; we see the chip of light, still now, waiting. Tycho makes himself bigger—a trick he has, like a bear— and puts himself between me and the light.

"Is it Pythias?" a familiar voice calls, before we can make out the speaker.

"Stop," Tycho orders the voice.

The lamp is held up to a face: Euphranor. "I'll walk you home," he says.

He goes in front and Tycho walks behind. At our door, Euphranor says, "I heard about your father."

I nod.

"Anything at all you need."

"Nothing," I say.

He bows and vanishes back into the trees, lamp extinguished now.

I give Tycho back his smelly wool, damp now, and he settles down in his sleeping spot. In my room I strip off my wet clothes and get into bed, where I sleep dreamlessly and wake clear-headed, my hair stiff with salt water. In the kitchen, Ambracis is serving Nico while Thale feeds the baby. Nico will leave as soon as he's finished breakfast.

I ask Ambracis to prepare me a bath.

"To prepare for your journey, Lady?" Thale says.

I give Nico some coins and tell him not to spend them all on cake.

"Come with me, Pytho," he pleads. "You can't stay here without money."

And weave in my room for the rest of my life, obeying Theophrastos? I indicate the coins. "I have money."

"You'll go to your mother, then?" Thale says. "In Stageira?"

The rustic life, far from books or even the possibility of books. I shake my head. "And what about Myrmex?" I ask. "If—*when* he comes back, where else will he come back to?"

"And if he doesn't?" Nico says.

"He will."

I walk Nico up to the garrison, where the leader is waiting for us. Nico is pale but contained; I'm proud of him. I tell him so, quietly, and he nods.

"Theophrastos loves you," I say.

"I know."

I kiss him, and he squeezes my hand. He won't hug me, not in front of all these soldiers. I expect them to show him to a cart, but Thaulos asks him if he'd like to ride. A horse is brought out, a lively, pretty thing. The men's faces soften when Nico's lights up.

He'll be fine.

I walk back to the house. Tycho goes in ahead of me while I linger outside in the garden, picking a few flowers for a vase for my room. Blue, purple, white. Athens, Stageira, Chalcis.

My husband will return, and then we'll see.

I go in and close the gate behind me. First, I'll have my bath.

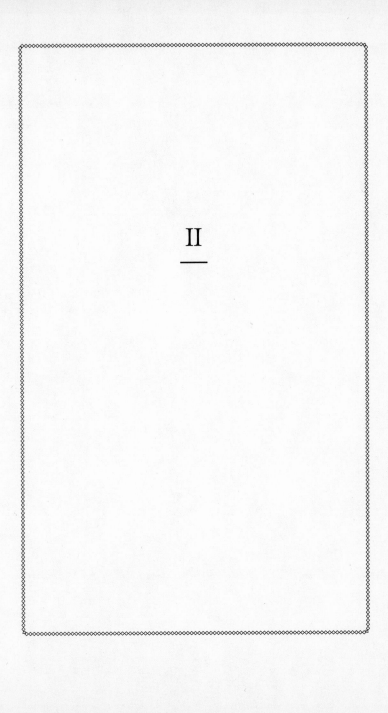

II

I'm in bed. When did that happen? Thale is sitting by me with her sweet old worried face, waiting to cluck and coo and spoon broth into me.

Sometimes I sleep.

It occurs to me that I'm alone.

I get up to use the pot and stagger, dizzy; arms catch mine on either side. I'm back in bed and there is a plate of fruit slices, a cup of milk. I would rather like a tonic, but there is no one to authorize that. I lie back and feel like a jellyfish, spreading and sinking into the bed. I cry very, very quietly but they catch me anyway. Gentle wiping of my face, a cool cloth for my forehead. My nose blown for me. *Blow, Lady*, like I'm three. Someone changes the sheets; someone changes me. I keep my eyes closed. Then I'm asleep for real.

Sometimes I forget. I forget the loss of them all for minutes at a time. The mouth in my stomach opens wide and yawns and I eat the fruit slices, take the spoonfuls of broth, sip at the milk. I'm surprised that no one is surprised by me, but then I remember they've spent years caring for Daddy, and must think I've fallen to his illness.

I start to think. There is the rational mind and the animal body. The animal body forces the thoughts away, does the forgetting; I'm ashamed how often the animal asserts itself. Food! Sleep! Rubbing the parts when Thale has gone to the kitchen for a minute! I understand, finally, that Daddy suffered so because he was practically all mind and no animal; he could never forget. I am lesser. Is it because I'm a girl? Daddy would say so. But that theory doesn't account for the animal natures of Nico, of Myrmex.

O Myrmex.

I get angry. How dare he betray us? How dare he leave me?

Then I'm up. I'm up and bathing and dressed and eating a fish on the stone terrace. I'm terribly thin; I hear Thale tell Simon. The baby smiles at me in big surprise and holds her arms up to me. Uppies, uppies! I pick her up. She kicks and squirms in the air for a moment, unsure, and then I bring her in to my chest for a hug. She touches my hair solemnly, touches my cheek. She looks into my eyes. Hers are brown, clean and clear. "Who's pretty?" I ask, and she says, "Me!"

Daddy's study is neat and tidy, and I'm not sure where to begin. I call Simon to help me. He shows me where Daddy kept the household accounts, and explains Herpyllis's system of the bowl on the high shelf with the money for marketing. I know that bowl. He suggests I write to Theophrastos about Myrmex's betrayal. He tells me today is a market day, and I give him money from my little purse. He hesitates.

"No meat," I tell him. He nods.

That is my first command as lady of the house.

I'm taking an inventory of the storeroom with Thale and

Ambracis when Tycho comes to say we have a visitor. *I have a visitor: Thaulos.* Tycho says he called twice while I was sick, but they sent him away.

I receive him in the formal front room. Ambracis brings a tray of walnuts and hot tea.

"Feeling better?" Thaulos asks. It's been a month since the reading of the will.

I bow my head, assenting in silence like a lady. *Silence garlands a woman and perfumes her.* I read that somewhere.

"I'm glad of it," he says. "I was sorry to hear of your condition. Nerves, was it?"

I bow my head.

"Nerves." He nods, pooching his lips judiciously, agreeing with his own diagnosis. "Well. You're getting the pink back, though, and that's what counts, eh?" He toasts me with his tea and winks.

Poor man. He must be terribly uncomfortable. I offer him a walnut.

"I'm afraid this isn't just a social visit." He inspects the walnut before he puts it in his mouth. Chews, swallows. Sips his tea. I'm doing very well so far. "I'm obliged to bring a financial concern to your attention. A rather pressing concern. Ah, gods." He puts a walnut back on the plate. "This is awful. Only it's about the house."

"This house?" I ask politely.

"There was supposed to be—" He looks vaguely around the room, clearly wishing there was someone else he could talk to, some man.

"Money?" I say.

He looks like I've slapped him.

"Is that the concern?"

He puts his cup on the table and leans forward. "You shouldn't have to deal with all this. You're just a child."

"There's no one else."

"The fellow in Athens, your father's—"

"There's no one else. How much do we owe?"

He doesn't answer.

"Myrmex told us he won the house in a bet," I say. "That must have been a lie. How much do I owe?"

He blinks, then tells me a sum.

"To you personally?"

He shakes his head. "To one of my officers. This was his house. I explained the situation to him and he was very—"

"Did Myrmex give him anything at all?"

He shows me his empty palms.

I look at my tea. Thinking thinking.

Thaulos says, "Perhaps I should be speaking with the boy himself, with—"

"Myrmex?"

"Does he have another name? 'Little Ant.' That's a child's nickname."

"That's what we've always called him," I say. *Jason* was for me and no one else; he never even told it to Herpyllis. "He's not here."

"Where is he?"

I explain and Thaulos listens. Sometimes I can see the father in him, sometimes the soldier. He stands. Perhaps the pettiness of our domestic relationships has disgusted him. "You need your father's man in Athens to act for you," he says. "And you need a husband. I'll send another request in dispatches to find out where your fellow is. What is he, infantry?"

"Cavalry."

He's looking around the room, at the furnishings. I send my mind chasing his, and then with a rush I pass him. "How much for a first payment?"

He's looking at a little ivory owl on a side table. He looks at me. I bow my head so I don't have to see him take it.

When I look up again he's on his feet. "You need to come up with the difference." His voice is harsh. He doesn't like taking owls from little girls. "If you don't come up with the difference, you'll have to leave. You understand it's a legal matter. I have no influence."

I bow my head.

"I want to help you, but I—"

Ambracis comes in with cheese.

"I'll be off." I stand to face him. "I'll be in touch about your intended. A word of advice. If that young man comes back—"

"Myrmex?"

"Act happy to see him, then send for me."

I thank him.

"And I'll send a courier tomorrow."

My face must be a question.

"For the next payment."

I bow my head in a fragrant silence.

❧

"And this is real Persian silk," the widow says. "Touch, go on. All these beautiful things are for enjoying. Sight is the least of the senses, I often think. We have tongues and toes and fingertips for a reason, no?"

She's already had me step out of my sandals so I can walk barefoot across a deep sheepskin rug. Now she's showing me a painted rose-silk curtain that falls from ceiling to floor. She coaxes it into my hands so I can feel the coolness of it; the tiny imperfections in the skin of my fingertips catch on the sheer surface. She takes the fabric back to rub against her cheek, then twirls her whole body in it. She makes me try. I feel the sheer cool all down the length of me, everything looking pink.

The house of Glycera smells of quince and spice. We settle into a private room, one wall open to a flower garden, for our weaving. She has a large cloth half done, and a new frame for me.

"Where are your daughters?" I ask.

She offers me a basket with many spools of coloured threads. I choose a blue. "I thought, for today, just you and me." She takes orange for herself and we begin. "How are you feeling?" she asks without looking up from her work.

It's the doorway I've been waiting for, the reason for my visit today. I tell her about Myrmex, and Thaulos, and the little owl, followed by the perfume bottle shaped like an almond, and the gold wire bracelet, and the new vase with the wrestlers on it— the one without the chip.

Glycera sets down her thread and looks at me. "You should have come to me three days ago." Cooler than I had expected, hoped.

"How do I find Myrmex?"

She does smile then, gently. "Sweetheart, you don't. He and that money are gone. *Why* do you not tell your father's man in Athens? Could he not pay?"

"He'd make me go live with him," I say. I realize how stupid an objection that sounds. "He doesn't like me. He thinks I talk too much. I'd have to spend all day indoors and eat with the women."

"That's all?" Glycera turns back to her weaving.

"He'd choose my books."

"And that's so important to you?"

I have to think about that. When did I last read a book?

"I think it is," she says. "I think it's very important to you."

"Is it?" I say. My face hurts, suddenly, from the effort of not crying.

"I can read, you know." She selects another thread, a rust. "My husband taught me. He liked me to read to him. And sing, and dance. And—talk, really. He loved to talk. We would have wonderful arguments about all sorts of things. Politics and ideas and art. You'd be surprised how many men prize an intelligent woman."

"Theophrastos doesn't."

"Then he's a boor." She sets her work down a second time and repeats the gesture from the party, lifting my chin with a single finger. "Your brows need tweezing."

She lies me down on a couch and sits beside me. She strokes my hair back from my forehead while we wait for the slave to fetch her tools. "So brown," she says. "You spend too much time in the sun. You've been a little wild thing all these years, haven't you? Going about on your own, swimming and reading books all day? Climbing trees, I don't doubt. Was it true, what your father said about healing that slave?"

I tell her it wasn't a bad infection and it probably would have healed itself. I was just a child, playing. The slave brings silver tweezers on a gold tray.

"No more talking now." She leans over me, so close I can feel her breath on my cheek. I close my eyes. She works quickly, expertly, the pinpricks arcing first below, then above the line of my brows. From time to time she presses a fingertip to my skin, firmly, to ease the pain. She smoothes a cool cream on after, for the redness.

"No, stay," she says, when I make to sit up. "I'm going to have a little lie-down, too." She takes the couch across the table from mine and together we contemplate the ceiling. "You asked about my daughters. Can I tell you a secret?"

The ceiling is painted blue with clouds. I'm not sure how to answer. "Yes," I say finally.

"I never had children," she says. "There was something wrong with me, inside. I took those girls in when they fell on hard times. Good girls, good families. But mistakes get made, accidents, misunderstandings, passions—fate can play with a young girl. As you yourself are discovering."

"Before your husband's death, or after?"

"After."

Her voice is light, high, girlish.

"I'm strict in some matters," she's saying. "My girls do as I tell them. I expect beauty and grace and cleanliness and hard work. But they are loved and cared for here. They have good food and lovely clothes and time to themselves to pursue their own interests. They have spending money and freedom, providing they use that freedom in a respectable way."

She sits up and looks at me and I understand that here comes the most important part. I sit up, too.

"All my girls can read," she says, reaching over to tap a finger on my knee. "You'd like it here."

I murmur appropriately, thanking her for her generosity, but demurring.

She cuts me off. "You don't understand," she says. "You'd be safe here."

I think for a moment, then lean forward to kiss her scented cheek.

When I pull back, her eyes are wet. "I know you're confused," she says. "Sweet girl. Think about it, that's all. And if you say no, I won't hold it against you. You'll still be welcome here. Your decisions are all your own, you see? That's what I've been trying to say."

I look at the loom she set up for me, the single line of blue all that I managed.

"I'll leave it there for you," she says. "For whenever you're ready."

"Thank you," I say again.

"Ah!" Her face lights up and she claps her hands. "Here is Meda to see you to the door."

Meda is the darkest-haired of the three, with the palest skin. I remember her from the women's room at the party. She drifts ahead of me, silently, in a dress of palest green gossamer that floats lightly behind her. Her scent is a trail of cinnamon I want to follow into a warm, dark forest, and sleep.

"Please come back," she says at the gate. "We get so lonely for visitors."

"What do you like to read?"

She smiles and touches her fingertips to her throat, *me?*

Tycho stands up from the shadows to escort me home.

※◎※

"Where does Master Euphranor live?" Tycho asks.

When he plays dumb like this, I want to hit him. "I have no idea," I say sweetly.

He stands there like a mule waiting for the whip.

"Ask at the garrison," I say. "Maybe he lives in barracks."

"Officers don't live in barracks."

"Tycho!"

"Lady," he says.

We stare at each other for a long moment. "Is there something you want to say?" I ask him.

"With your permission."

I nod.

"Your father would have wanted you to be with your brother."

"And Theophrastos."

He nods.

"My father took an interest in the farm. He wanted to visit it himself. He thought it could be made more profitable. I'm doing what my father intended to do."

"What he intended for himself," Tycho says.

"Yes," I say. "Let me know when you've returned. With a reply."

He picks my letter up from the table. "What if I can't—"

"Tycho!"

He goes.

Then it's morning, the next morning, and we're riding, Euphranor and I, he on his black beast and me on Spiffy, under the skeletal black trees on the long lane to the farms. The horses' hooves ring out on the frozen ground. I feel the fizz in me, the wine in my blood. We've left the cart with the lunch and the slaves far behind. He's quiet today, Euphranor, none of the jolly hostliness he patronized Daddy with. That suits me well enough. He smiles tentatively at me from time to time and I think he has a nice face. I like that he knows how to be quiet.

We stop at the entrance to the yard, familiar now: his own farm. Demetrios doesn't appear. Euphranor doesn't move to dismount or make any suggestion at all, so we just sit, silently, resting the horses. Curiosity, that fine edge, is blunted in me since Daddy's death, an irony I'm not curious enough to puzzle through. I sit feeling sad in the bright cold air, the wind moving a few dead, clinging leaves high, high up in the trees. From far away comes the sound of footsteps on gravel, running. Closer and closer. Neither of us moves or looks at the other; I like that.

Tycho appears through the trees. He stops a dozen paces away and simply stands, breathing heavily. Nothing to deliver, nothing to say. I understand he didn't like letting me out of his sight, didn't like me riding with Euphranor unescorted. I understand and dismiss the understanding, let it float out of my mind like fumes. It's not his place to worry about such things, and beneath me to notice a slave's worry. I will let it go.

"We're just over here," Euphranor says, as though he's received some signal I can't hear, like a dog. He's let Tycho catch his breath. Another thought I allow to float away. Noticing an officer noticing a slave, and liking that about him, disliking myself for liking that—it's all too complicated. I open my mind's hand and release the thought like a birdie. *Fly away, don't bother me.*

We ride a few hundred paces farther down the lane to the derelict property we would have visited had Daddy not twisted his ankle. I understand—without surprise, in my dream-like state—this place is Daddy's. Is mine. The shack in the yard has a staved-in roof. The fields are choked with dead grass. If the place has borne a crop in the last ten years, there's no evidence of it.

Euphranor helps me down from Spiffy and hands the reins to Tycho. We walk a little way into the yard. No flowers, no herbs, no kitchen patch. No hens, no pigs, no goats, no berries, no vines, no rustics working the fields, no country girls singing over their tasks. It's winter, of course, but metaphorically.

"It's bad," I say to Euphranor.

He walks around the shack, kicking the foundation stones, peering in the black windows.

"How long has it been like this?"

He waves me over. Through the window I see yellow grass longer than my hair, sprouting in the corners.

"I've done what I can, over the years," he says. "We used to bring in the fruit before the trees went bad. Demetrios tried to harvest the fields one year, but it was too much work. It's a big property. You need someone here full-time."

"I thought there was."

Euphranor gestures at the shack.

"I don't think Daddy knew."

"Not a worldly man," Euphranor says. Commiseration or contempt? "The foundation's still solid. First thing is, you get that roof fixed and get someone living in here."

"A caretaker," I say.

"A farmer." Euphranor gives me a look, long and clear and cool as water. "You want to turn a profit as quickly as possible, yes?"

Behind us, the remaining slaves have trundled into the yard with the cart, and are awaiting instruction.

"Do you have someone in mind?"

He shrugs. "I said it was too much work for Demetrios. That's without recompense, you understand. We might come to an arrangement."

"I don't understand." I kick a dead leaf from my foot reflexively. "You never made this offer to Daddy? How's he had income from the farm all these years if it's been like this?"

"Maybe he was muddled," Euphranor says. "Some men aren't careful with money, particularly if they have it coming in from many sources. It probably just got lost in the accounts."

"You never wrote to him?" I persist.

"I never knew who owned the place until your family arrived in Chalcis. Don't be angry at *me*, girl. I'm trying to help."

O he should not have called me that.

"I know the situation you're in," he says. "These things get around. I don't really see how you've got a choice."

I understand he's taking the farm.

"Are there outbuildings?"

"Worse than this." He kicks the foundation, again. I want to say, *Excuse me, please, but you don't kick that. That's mine.* "You can't live here," he says, reading my mind.

"Equipment?"

"Stolen." He nods. "I remember, a couple of years back, Demetrios telling me he'd checked the barn one day and everything was gone." He holds my look, daring me to challenge him. I know where the equipment is, and he knows I know.

"I'll buy new."

"What will you buy?" Of course I have no idea. "There's no seed, either," he says when I don't answer. "Must have been stolen at the same time."

"Must have been," I say.

We look at each other.

"Which bedroom did you take?" he asks. "The birds, or the butterflies?"

I close my eyes, open them.

"I've been kind to your family," he says softly, though there's no one but slaves to overhear. "I was assured your people were—solvent. It's a big house for one man, but I'm fond of it all the same. I've given you more than enough time to grieve. Any court would say I'd be well within my rights to take it back."

Any court is Plios, the magistrate. I could risk it, maybe.

Suddenly Euphranor's mood seems to shift. "Don't let's

fight," he says. "We should eat, instead. Things always look better on a full stomach. Come on, little one, don't look so gloomy. I'm trying to be nice to you. Still fancy that swim? I sent ahead to have Demetrios clear the pond."

"No, thank you," I say. "It's too cold."

"Oh, but I know how you love to swim."

The tone of his voice.

"You have a birthmark, lighter skin rather than darker. Just here." He touches himself. "I understand those are quite rare, the light ones. Quite—distinctive."

I blush, as he intends.

We ride back to his farm, where the slaves lay out the picnic on a table in the yard. We eat.

"Have Thaulos stop sending his couriers, then," I say.

Triumph; but he takes it quietly. "Actually, that's out of my hands." He doesn't look up from his bread. "He *was* promised a—gift, shall we say, to arrange things. By that brother of yours. The one who fancied himself a gambler."

"How big a gift?"

Euphranor tells me he'll make enquiries, and see if he can negotiate a settlement on my behalf. As the slaves are packing up, he says, "Sure you don't want that swim?"

My first kiss, there in the yard, so quick the slaves don't even look up. I manage to twirl out of it, like Glycera in the silk.

"Birds or butterflies?" he whispers.

I wipe my lips hard on the back of my hand and he smiles, but sadly. Odd.

I'm marked, now; his ghostmark on my mouth. My lips go chapped from all my licking, trying to get it off. Another loss to grieve: the first kiss should have been my husband's. Probably I'm spoiled now, and my husband will know it; he'll smell it on me. But by the time I'm his to taste, the ceremony will be over, we'll already be married, and I'll be safe. He'll be angry, though. Perhaps the way to do it will be to make sure he drinks a lot of wine, so that he won't even notice. If we can get past the first moment, then he'll have marked me with his own scent, and he'll never have to know.

I look at my mouth in the little bronze Herpyllis gave me, this way and that. Morning bounces off it onto the walls.

"Lady." Thale taps on my door frame. "The courier is here."

I hand her the bronze and tell her to give it to him. She frowns. "He'll understand," I say.

After the clop of hooves has faded away, Thale returns.

"You may speak," I say.

She suggests a visit to the temple. A thread of iron firms her jaw, and she's piled her hair on the back of her head in the style called the melon, instead of her usual skinned-back pinning. She wears her best dress, a wheat-coloured wool I remember Herpyllis sewing her for a gift. I wonder if she misses Herpyllis. She whispers, "For guidance."

I know she favours Aphrodite, but I don't.

"Tell Tycho." I get off my bed and look around for clothes. My room's a mess, lately. Thale touches her hair, meaning mine, so I let her comb it quickly and whip it into a loose approximation of her own. "What shall we take?"

Thale shows me her own offering, a pair of sandals the baby has outgrown.

"Let's take Pretty with us," I say. "She'll enjoy the walk."

Thale takes a deep breath and doesn't exhale. The next moment, she's gone to fetch her from Olympios. She'll never have a baby of her own; my father told me years ago she was too old. She's shy around Olympios's baby; awed, I think. The little girl never naturally reached for Thale, with her hard sharp angles and her nervousness and her onion smell. Thale will adore a morning of holding her chubby little hand and wiping her mouth.

In the courtyard, Olympios is lingering, making a show of sweeping the already clean ground. He looks grim. The baby is clean and neatly dressed; her hair is up. She looks serious. Olympios kneels to say a word in her ear, while Thale waits for the handover. She's practically vibrating.

I hold my hand out to the baby. "Shall we go for a walk, Pretty?"

She takes my hand on one side and Thale's on the other.

"Don't let her run away," Olympios says, so soft and terrified an order that I don't reprimand him. Tycho catches his eye and nods, and Olympios nods back. They're both such big men; I shouldn't want to laugh at their concern over a tiny girl, but I do.

Pretty walks very nicely all the way to the temple of Artemis. My choice—huntress, virgin, patron of young girls. She watches Thale leave the sandals in the massive votive pile by the gate, and unclutches her little fist to reveal her own offering: a wooden bead Olympios must have given her. Gravely she lays it next to the sandals. Both of them turn enquiringly to me.

"Take Pretty to see the lamps," I tell Thale.

When they're gone, I draw the last black hair from my pouch. I only burned two for the iunx; the third I kept, just to keep. I lay it next to Pretty's bead, where the shadows swallow it; I blink and it's gone.

"The goddess will understand, I suppose?"

A priestess. I jump, startled.

"May I make a suggestion?" Not just any priestess; the head priestess, she of the black brows, from Plios's party. "Next time, you might tie it to something so it doesn't get lost. Something shiny, to attract the goddess's attention."

"A coin, perhaps."

The priestess gestures elegantly, as though to say that's none of her business; she's above such worldly concerns. I reach back into my pouch and add a coin to the pile.

She tells me she's reading one of Daddy's books, and is learning so much. She confesses she was unfamiliar with his work before we came to Chalcis, and regrets now she did not take advantage of his acquaintance while he was alive.

"Which book?"

"The *Prior Analytics*. Oh, it's beautiful. Elegant."

"Difficult," I say, in case she finds it so.

Her face lights with interest. "You've read it?"

"I've read all my father's work."

Her hands float into the air, fingers fluttering, a mannerism I'll get to know well. It means excitement, anticipation. "But that's marvellous! And you write, too?"

"I do."

A child's voice, rising. *No, no, no!* The priestess of Artemis and I flinch simultaneously, then smile at the mirror image we make. "The goddess loves children," the priestess says. "It's a dreadful failing of mine that I so wish her supplicants would leave them at home."

I bite back a laugh.

"Unusual young woman," she says, not disapproving. "We're not all cut out for the family life, you know."

*No, no, no! Bad Thale!*

I catch Thale's eye, where she's struggling to keep Pretty from touching the lamps, and look sharply at the door. *Take her out.*

The priestess follows my glance, and looks back to me enquiringly.

"Members of my household," I say. "The child has never been to the temple. I apologize, I apologize. She's usually very well behaved."

Thale stoops to pick up Pretty, who's now lying on the floor, and gets a kick to the face. The priestess gestures to an attendant, who scoops up the now shrieking girl and takes her outside, trailing the weeping Thale. I touch the pain budding at my temple.

"As I was saying." With her toe, the priestess nudges into alignment the sandals, the bead, the coin. "We were not all made for the family life. Some of us need more silence, more contemplation. Devotion can take many forms, yes?"

I'm distracted by a procession of girls in matching dresses carrying votive offerings from the pile to, presumably, a storeroom in the complex of sanctuary buildings behind the temple. Young priestesses.

"Will you come and visit me again? By yourself, next time, perhaps, so you can spend more time on your contemplations?" The priestess's gaze follows mine. "I could introduce you to some of the young women who serve the goddess here. They could tell you about their lives. Might you like to know more about their lives?"

I nod, slowly. From outside rises a high, thin wail like the blade of a knife.

The priestess stoops to pick up my coin. "I think someone needs a sweet." She hands the coin back to me. "One's first visit to the temple should be an occasion of joy. A honey-cake from the market to sweeten the memory."

I take the coin slowly.

The priestess winks. "Go on. The goddess and I are old friends. I'll explain it to her. Will you come again?"

"I will," I say. Then, more warmly: "I will."

She smiles.

9⊛8

At home there is meat for supper; Simon and Thale, who eat with me, won't meet my eye. I don't ask. Meat, and bread and wine. I don't call it tonic anymore. It's just wine, and I drink it, properly watered, like Herpyllis did every supper time. I'm a lady now.

The next morning, I give the courier my gold bracelet with the ram's-head clasp, the one Daddy gave me. The next night there is meat again. Leftovers from the night before, must be.

"Beans tomorrow," I tell Thale, just to be sure.

"I don't like beans," she says.

She's clearing the table, just as always, and I watch her until I'm pretty sure I only imagined what she said. A bone slips from a plate onto the ground, and she doesn't pick it up. The puppy—not so little anymore—comes nosing over and gnaws at it until it starts to cough. Nico wanted to take it to Athens with him, but we guessed he belonged with the house. I get the bone away and hold it out to Simon, who pretends he doesn't see. He turns away to follow Thale to the kitchen. I put the bone on the table.

I'm cold.

In bed I pile on all my furs and lie curled tight, toes tucked behind a knee to keep them warm. Much later, deep in the night, a woman's laugh wakes me. A lovely, low, warm, tickling laugh. I know what it means; but who?

The courier arrives again while I'm eating breakfast; Simon brings him to me. "No," I say. "Yesterday was for two days. Two days at least. Probably three, probably more."

The courier says nothing, doesn't move.

"You go back and tell your master what I said."

He doesn't move.

"Go," Simon says.

He goes.

When I open my mouth to thank Simon, he cuts me off by asking what I'll give tomorrow.

I open my mouth, change my mind. "More jewellery."

"Show it to me."

An order? I raise my eyebrows.

"If you're going to give it away, you might as well get the proper value of it. Give it to me and I'll change it to cash in the market."

"I should have thought of that."

"They'd cheat you there too. Let me see to it."

I think about that.

"Bring it out," he says. "Show me."

Then I'm showing him my special box, and he's stirring through it with one thick dirty finger. He picks out a few things.

"No," I say softly. My baby necklace with the gold wire flowers, the one from my mother.

"We need to eat."

I hold out my hand, shaking. He hesitates long enough to show me who's making the decision.

"Just that one," I say, and he gives me back the necklace. One of the flowers is already bent from its brief stay in his fist.

"Selfish little girl," he whispers.

*Yes.*

⁙

Over the days that follow, objects start to disappear: metals first, carvings, pots. Or have they been gone for a while and I'm only noticing now? I check the storeroom to find the winter stores alarmingly depleted; where is it all going? Then, one night, Thale brings me beans and serves herself meat. We're sitting inside, in the room for guests; it's too cold for the courtyard.

"We don't eat meat every night in this house," I say.

"You have what you wanted."

I stand. "You wouldn't have treated Herpyllis this way."

"Herpyllis is gone." She eats doggedly, without looking at me.

In the kitchen I find the slaves, also eating meat. Only Tycho stands when he sees me. I realize, with a kind of animal instinct, it would be wrong to show anger or distress of any kind. "Where's Simon?" I say instead.

Tycho leads me to the stables, where Simon is plucking a goose.

"That money was for the house," I say right away when I see him.

Simon shrugs.

"These aren't your decisions."

Simon says nothing. I feel Tycho, behind me, getting bigger.

"Was that Thale's goose?" I squint at it. "The egg goose? Why would you do that?"

I'm not here, apparently; Simon continues as though I'm just a breeze passing through.

In the courtyard, Tycho clears his throat.

"You may speak," I say.

"Your father believed too much meat to be unhealthy for the digestion."

I blink. "Yes. I know."

"You must stop them."

I touch my temple. "Yes."

He says no more, and I assume he's done. I turn away, but he doesn't follow.

"Yes," I say.

"Ambracis has a visitor," he says. "At night."

It's my turn to say nothing.

"From the house of Agapios." Our near neighbours. "One of the servant boys there. I've caught Philo spying on them."

My mind, unbidden, performs its trick of outracing his; I see Philo peeking through a curtain, rubbing himself; hear again Ambracis's laugh.

"Is she happy?" I ask.

"During the day Philo is at her, now. At her all the time. We don't know what to do."

"Keep them apart."

Tycho hesitates; nods. I go to my room with a massive pain behind my eyes, leaving the servants to their feast. Tomorrow, I will seize everything back.

The next morning, Ambracis's eyes are red and her face is bloated from weeping. She slaps my plate in front of me—dry bread—and stares at me with sheer hatred.

"Philo," I tell Tycho, when he answers my summons. "Keep *Philo* away from her, I meant. Not the other one. I don't care what she does with the other one."

Tycho frowns.

"Oh, what now?" I snap.

"Your father never permitted lewdness amongst the servants."

*Herpyllis was a servant*, I want to say. Instead I tell him I intend to spend the morning in my father's study, reading, and am not to be disturbed.

"May I eat now, Lady?" he asks.

"What?"

"With your permission."

"You don't need my permission."

"Bread and water, no more."

I wonder if Tycho is losing his mind.

"With your permission," he insists.

"Of course you have my permission." I shoo him away with my hand, the way my father used to when he was irritable.

This becomes a new, supremely annoying habit of his: asking permission before every meal. I understand he means to set some kind of example—for the other servants, for me— but his displays of meagre eating grate on me even more than the others' new-found passion for meat.

I spend the next day in my father's study. I'm reading the *Odyssey*, of course, reading and rereading the part about the suitors eating Penelope out of house and home while her men are away.

Finally I take up pen and paper and write the letter I've been avoiding. Salutations to my father's most esteemed colleague, gratitude for all his assistance, much affection to my little brother, and could Theophrastos offer news of the political situation? Was there the possibility of a visit? Me to him, him to me?

I send Simon on Spiffy. I intuit—correctly—a trip to Athens will appeal to him. And he likes Nico. Everyone likes Nico.

He's back, not the next night, but the one after.

Salutations to the child of his esteemed and honoured teacher, the letter says, political situation too complex to explain, ongoing attacks on Macedonian citizens, at all costs the child of his esteemed and honoured teacher should remain where she is; unsafe for her to travel.

But *you* are not Macedonian, Theophrastos; and what of Nico?

He wants me to say it straight out, I think, that I can't manage by myself. He's read Simon, the spite and the insolence in the line of his spine and the curl of his lip. He knows, he knows, and he'll let me suffer on a little more. He's punishing me for all the times I teased him about his books.

I drop the letter in the brazier. So.

%

A hot dream of wetness and lust, hips in a rhythm, someone moaning, and then Tycho is by my bed, touching my shoulder. *Lady, Lady.*

"Ambracis?" I say.

I follow him to the receiving room, where a big male slave waits. "My lady Glycera requires you," the new one says.

"Where's Ambracis?"

Tycho shakes his head; doesn't know.

"Thale?"

Tycho looks at the floor.

"I see," I say weakly. Animals, all of them, their lusts shimmering in the air all through the house and invading my dreams. And poor Tycho having to look and look for a woman to wake me, having to spy them at it, and finally having to get me himself and risk a whipping. I tell him, "It's all right."

"My lady says quickly," the new slave says.

Tycho looks straight at me and shakes his head, minimally.

"I beg your pardon?"

"Now." The big slave's face is bold. "She says you're to come now."

"It's the middle of the night."

"She'll be dead by morning."

I'm so tired.

"Not my lady. The young one."

"I don't understand."

The big slave actually turns and leaves the house, running home, I suppose, now that his message is delivered. And I'd go back to bed, too, if Tycho doesn't say, "It's not safe," so then of course I have to defy him and go.

We're in the street, me a little bear beside him in my furs, my breath white in the moonlight. Ice crusts the ground. Tycho walks slower and slower until finally he says, "Not this house."

We've arrived.

Tycho says, "It's a whorehouse, Lady. Everyone knows."

Someone screams inside.

"You could sell me," Tycho says.

"Don't tell me what to do," I say. "Nobody would want you, anyway. Wait here."

The big slave is waiting in the doorway. We leave Tycho behind and he leads me to a room pulsing with light and pain. Lamps lamps lamps and a girl on the bed. So many women crammed in the tiny room, so many scents all clashing in panic. The girl on the bed is naked and the baby is coming. My dream, so.

What would my father do.

"Out." I point at one girl after another. "Out, out, out."

As they flee, one steps forward. She's not like the others: scrubbed face, homely clothes, smelling of herself. She tells me she's the midwife. I see in her face judgment of me withheld. "Let me stay," she says.

I nod. There are just four of us in the room now: the girl, the midwife, me, and the woman who hasn't left, the one I can't order about. "How is she?"

"Thank you," Glycera says.

The girl screams again as the pains surge. The midwife puts a hand between the legs, checking something.

"She didn't look pregnant," I say.

"She wore a corset," Glycera says.

The midwife makes a face. "You could have hurt the baby," I say. "You must never corset a pregnant woman. My father taught me that."

"Your father is here to help us now," Glycera says to me. "I feel it. All right, now, Meda. All right. Look who we've brought to help us. It'll all be over soon."

I look at the midwife, who makes a wry face.

"I'm Pythias," I say to her. "What's your name?"

"Clea."

The girl screams at a new pitch. Something inside her is changing.

"She started early this morning," Clea the midwife says. "Want a look?"

She's twice my age, and tolerating me with a patience that tells me there's no real danger; I can't understand why Glycera summoned me. I ask Glycera for clean towels and she hurries out.

"Her daughter," I say.

"Her something." Clea shows me the dark hot mess between

the girl's legs, the pee smell and the blood and the drenched black curls. Expertly she inserts her fingers. "She's doing fine."

The girl throws up just as Glycera returns with the towels. "Water," I tell her, and she goes back out. I clean up the vomit and wipe the girl's face.

The midwife has stationed herself at the end of the bed, between the girl's legs. "We're going to push soon," she tells me.

"Meda," I say loudly. "We're going to push, Meda."

"Like using the pot," Clea says.

"Like using the pot," I tell Meda. "You're going to push like you're using the pot. Can you do that?"

"Yes," the girl says.

"When the next pain comes." Clea touches her belly, looks down below. "Ready?"

The girl screams and pushes. I feel Glycera's shadow in the doorway, but she doesn't come in. "Good, Meda, good!" I say.

"Two or three more like that," Clea says.

She pushes again as the next pains come: two, three, four times. Clea dips her fingers in a dish on the floor and massages where the baby's coming. When she sees me looking, she explains. "Olive oil."

The girl screams again and Clea's face changes; I can tell she's got the head. Joy, briefly, then not. "Once more," she tells the girl.

And the baby slides out wet and blue and cheesy. "Take it," Clea barks. I hold out a towel to receive the baby while Clea cuts the cord. It's turning pink already. It's big and has a mat of black hair. Wide blue eyes. An innocent pink snarl: a harelip.

"Pretty boy," I say, "pretty boy," for Meda to hear, and Clea for the first time shoots me a poisonous look. I hold the baby while she finishes with the girl, the cord and the afterbirth, and then she takes the baby back from me. "Clean her up, will you?" she says. To Glycera: "Lady, your daughter is thirsty."

Glycera disappears a third time.

I change the sheets and swab the blood from Meda. I wrap her in clean things and wipe her face again, and kiss her cheek, and tell her she's done very, very well. The baby goes quiet. When I turn back to Clea, she's got the baby swathed head to toe so you can't see any part of him. Even his face.

Glycera drops the cup in the doorway.

"Stillborn," Clea says. "I'm so sorry."

Glycera starts to cry. She sits on the bed next to Meda and takes her in her arms and they cry together, racking sobs.

"No," I say. I feel logic in me, cold and strong, pushing down everything else. "No."

Clea uncovers the baby's face to show me. I touch the cheek. Clea has cleaned him; no more mucus, no more cheese. She holds the little body out and I take it. I press my cheek to the little dead one, still warm.

Clea says, "Cry. Let it out." But nothing comes out of me.

We leave Glycera and Meda in the room. Clea carries the baby clutched to her chest like it's still alive. Tycho stands when he sees us.

"Where will you take it?" I ask.

The midwife shakes her head.

"Why?"

"He couldn't have latched on to the breast. He would have starved. This was quicker. Kinder."

"You don't know that."

"I do, Pythias." She tries to smile and I see that, like me, she is crying all over the inside of her face. "I've seen it many, many times. You were a great help to me tonight. I thought my lady had lost her reason, calling you, but she's always proved herself an astute judge of character. Always, and she wasn't wrong about you either. Your grandfather was a doctor, she told me."

I say, "You've helped Glycera's daughters—many times, then?"

"Many times."

"Where will you take him?"

She looks at me for a long moment.

"I'll bury him," she says simply. "With a friend. He won't be alone."

AT THE GATES TO ARTEMIS's sanctuary, I tell Tycho to go back to the house. "Mule!" I say, when he doesn't move.

"Yes, Lady."

"Go!"

"Yes, Lady."

He stands lumpishly until a light approaches from deep in the complex. The head priestess holds a lamp up, her face an enquiry. I can tell she was sleeping.

"Make him go." I wipe my wet face with the back of my hand. "Make him go."

She does something to the inside of the gate and it opens enough to admit me to the outer sanctuary. She closes it quickly again behind me, though Tycho doesn't move.

"Go!" I order one more time, harsh as I can, and that is the last I see of him for many days.

"You're bleeding." The priestess leads me to an alcove, where she lights more lamps from the one she's holding. My clothes are bloody from the birth and I smell of Meda's vomit. "Who did this to you?"

"No one."

More priestesses appear, silently. They want to bathe me before I go inside; then they want me to sit on the steps by the goddess and recover myself that way. I tell them what *I* want.

"Indeed." The priestess who admitted me takes my hands in hers, looks at them. Filthy. "One of your slaves?"

I shake my head.

"The baby died?"

I don't answer.

"Yes." She smoothes my hair back from my face, like Herpyllis used to. "It hurts everywhere, doesn't it?"

I spend the night on a cot in the alcove, attended by the head priestess herself. She sits by me, sometimes humming a little. She has a husband and three children at home, she tells me; she had to send a slave to tell her household she'd be away for the night. She inherited the priesthood from her mother and her grandmother before her. I try to imagine her down on the rug in front of her hearth, playing horsey, giggling with her sons. She has a kind, tired face. "I thought you disliked children," I say. "That day I first came to the temple—"

"I thought that was what you needed to hear. Sleep, now."

The next morning, she takes me into the room where they bathe and tells me to take off my clothes. She walks a circle around, tapping her lips with her fingers, while two other priestesses stand ready to assist her.

"What's this?" she asks of the scar Myrmex gave me on my thumb.

"My brother and I were fighting. It was an accident."

She runs her finger along it. "That must have hurt."

"No."

Around and around she goes. "Any pains anywhere? Ever been sick as a child, really sick? Ever had an injury?" No, no, no. "Are you a virgin?" Yes. "Will you let me see?" Yes. I lie down on a blanket the attendants spread for me, and spread my legs. She kneels down and peers.

"I didn't know you could tell that by looking," I say.

"The hole goes slack when it's used." She stands and signals I may do the same. The attendants give me back my clothes.

"It doesn't matter so much, really, virginity," the priestess says while she waits for me to dress. "We're obliged to check, but it doesn't really affect what you can do here. I think perhaps in the old days it mattered more. One of those old traditions we cling to, yes? But perhaps without meaning, in the modern world."

"I love the old traditions," I say, because I guess she does, too.

"You were honest with me, anyway," she replies. "That matters more."

We return to the big room, where a committee has assembled. The head priestess announces I am whole. "No significant blemishes, no scars. All fingers and toes."

"Not beautiful," another says. "But perhaps she can be made so."

"Clear skin," a third says. "Dark, though. She'll need powder."

Next, we talk about money. Normally my family would be expected to buy me the kind of position I'm asking for.

"Her father was renowned," the head priestess says. "She brings prestige."

They spend some time discussing my role in the life of the cult. Weaving, water-bearing, fire-tending, cooking, cleaning; each a sacred ritual. Holy housework. They decide on water-bearing. Because I have no cash in hand to purchase my position, I'm in no position to choose.

No one asks about the household I've abandoned.

✸

The work is unexpectedly hard and I lose myself in it. I talk as little as possible. The goddess is a lamp in a labyrinth; I can't think about the darkness that is her absence. It hurts to think about much at all. My hands blister and peel; I bind them with rags and keep working. There's a spring behind the temple, and I spend my days carrying pots back and forth. I wear a ponytail and a knee-length dress and boots, like the goddess. In the evenings I sit on the steps at her feet, gazing at her. The priestesses have sewn her a dress of fawn-skin and she carries a fine bow and leather quiver of arrows. Huntress, virgin, goddess of the moon. And of childbirth.

At night, when the other priestesses are asleep, I ask her why the baby had to die. Her face is stern. I tell her they could have given him a chance to suck, they could have fed him from a spoon. Couldn't they have fed him from a spoon?

*Babies drink a drop at a time,* she tells me. *Their tummies are the size of grapes. He would have choked off a spoon. You know this.*

I've seen adults with harelips, though. Some of them must survive.

*Many more die of starvation.* Now her face is sad. *Have you seen a baby die of starvation? Have you heard one cry and then cry less? I have. You know it can take a week or more?*

She wants my tears, I think sometimes. I give them to her, weep on her feet and don't wipe them away. She puts pictures in my head and takes her price. During the day, mothers bring their sick babies to her. They leave offerings, all kinds of things. There's no set price. Gold, cloth, meat, leather, pots, coins, jewellery, beans, oil, perfume, cosmetics, knives, wheat, corn, paper, musical instruments, tools. If they can write, they write notes. The older priestesses take these things to the storeroom, a room I've never entered. They sew clothes for the goddess, wash and change her every few days. They put cosmetics on her face, anoint her, scent her, polish the gold chains that bind her hair, rub her tired feet, oil the leather quiver to keep it supple. On holy days she wears purple. I've seen her naked, all white marble and ivory, and find her most beautiful then, though the making and mending and cleaning of her clothes is one of the highest callings in the cult.

"You're happy here," the head priestess says to me one day. "Content."

"Yes."

"You work hard. I've been watching you." She picks up my hands to look at them as she did the first night. Bound now in rags. "The goddess is pleased with you."

"I love her."

The head priestess nods. We affect the seriousness of the goddess, we priestesses, and rarely smile. I hope my cousin will come to Chalcis soon. He'll pay the debt and understand that I belong to the goddess now, and can never leave the temple. Marriage is out of the question. He'll feel the spark of her in me when he touches me. He'll burn his hands. He'll understand.

At night she whispers to me and touches me. I can't make out the words. She comes when I'm almost asleep, when I'm about to let go. She tells me the baby is in another place. He can smile, now, and laugh, and gum a rusk, and drink from a cup. He has a puppy to cuddle and sleep with. She strokes my hair and kisses my cheek and holds me until I'm asleep.

I wake one night to use the pot and hear women's voices from the storeroom, hear laughter, and see light outlining the door. I go closer. Through the crack I see the priestesses filling sacks with the votive offerings.

"No, that's mine," one of them says, snatching a gold bracelet from her sister's hand. "You always take the best for yourself."

"I have four children," the other whines. "You only have two. They're expensive to feed."

"Take the meat, then," the first one says.

"It's already high."

"The salt fish."

"Oh, the salt fish. They're sick of salt fish." She makes another grab for the bracelet, but the first priestess is taller, and holds it out of her reach. The others laugh.

In the morning I ask the head priestess about what I saw. She tells me I was dreaming.

"No," I say. "I wasn't dreaming."

We sit at the goddess's feet.

"Think, Pythias," she begins. "Think about how things were when you were a baby, a toddler. Think about the people who mattered most to you. Your father, your mother, your nurse. Your love for them was huge and simple. Your love was a massive block of uncut stone. It was featureless, and nothing could shift it."

That's beautiful.

"Now think, Pythias. Think on a few years. You're a little girl now. You like some foods better than others, some toys better than others, some people better than others. You remember?"

I remember.

"That big block of stone, it's chipped away a little now at the edges. It's starting to take on a form."

It's smaller.

"It's more refined. More interesting. Now you're of age. What does the block look like now? You chip away and chip away, don't you? It takes almost all your time, all your days. You're working at it in a fever. What does it look like now?"

I look at the goddess.

"Yes," she says. "It could end up looking like her. One of her servants. Or it could end up looking like something else entirely. *You* could end up as something else entirely. Something not so lovely, maybe."

"Are you threatening me?"

She smiles. "Just a little. You have to understand, it's a privilege to be here. Would you abuse that privilege?"

"Have I?"

She pats my knee. "Only with the tip of your big toe."

"Because of what I saw?"

"Even once you've carved your stone," she says, as though she hasn't heard me, "you keep chipping away. Your love for your parents changed, didn't it, over time?"

I think about that.

"Your love for the goddess will change, too. Life is long, Pythias. Over time your love will grow deeper, or smoother, or however you'd like to imagine it."

"My father," I say slowly, "would have said you were telling yourself a pretty story to make your life bearable. That there are no gods, no blocks of marble."

"No parents?" the head priestess says, still smiling. "No children? No love?"

"It's not *such* a pretty story, surely. To think that we're all chipping away, chipping away, our loves getting smaller and smaller until we die. Is that really what you believe?"

She shrugs. "I believe in change. I believe love changes over time."

"Even for her?" I point my chin at the goddess.

"Even for her."

"Grows less."

"Grows different." She stands. "Becomes clearer."

"And deeper, and smoother."

We're both standing, facing each other now. Fighting stance.

"More forgiving," she says. "We're not very forgiving, when we're young."

"What should I be forgiving?"

She puts her palm to my cheek.

Hours later, the goddess is pale in the moonlight. I tell her I've always been lonely.

*So have I.*

Even with so many to care for you?

*Even so.*

Are my sisters in the storeroom?

*Go see.*

The baby, I say, tell me some more about the baby.

*He's sleeping.*

She's so lovely, adorned in moonlight. She needs nothing else. I reach up to finger the hem of her short dress.

*Go see.*

I tell her I don't want to leave her.

*You will leave me,* she says. *And another will take your place.*

No.

*They wear my jewels,* she says. *They try on my clothes. They eat my meat and drink my wine. They perfume themselves and make themselves lovely in my image. They hide my gold in their clothes and give it to their families. Where else do you think my offerings go?*

No.

*You've always known.*

No.

*You can do the same.*

No!

*Child,* she says. *Let me care for you. Let me feed you and clothe you. Let me shelter you. Let me love you.*

I put my hands over my ears.

*Daughter,* she says. I can still hear her, long after I've left the temple and am running, running, trailing the spark of her until it's extinguished behind me.

The house is cold.

Leaves have drifted into the rooms from outside. The walls are cold to touch, and damp; my fingers leave snail trails of the thinnest wet. A chair lies on its side in the inner courtyard, in front of a table crowded with empty wine cups: someone's party ended clumsily. There's no one in the kitchen, though the tables are crammed with dirty dishes. There's green scum in more than one bowl. The door to the storeroom hangs by a single hinge to reveal chaos inside, food looted and spilled. What is there to feel? They left me; I left them. We're all fending for ourselves now.

Someone is saying words in one of the rooms. Daddy's room. Primly, my ears refuse the shape of these words, keys that won't fit those locks. I follow the sound of them, though, and hold the heavy curtain far enough to one side, with a single finger, to see their fierce proclaimer: Thale, naked on the bed, Simon holding her ankles in the air at an angle that must—at her age—hurt. He's pumping her. I let the curtain go but what I've seen will stay with me for hours, flashing like after-images when you've stared at the sun: the meat of his back, the slop of her breasts, their open mouths, the rhubarb-y business I glimpse between Simon's legs on the out-stroke. Thale's hair on Daddy's pillow, and the filth she's spewing into the air he breathed when he slept, the self-same pocket of breath.

I understand only slowly that Thale is experiencing great pleasure.

I back away, then turn and—what? I don't run, because I can't feel my feet. I am soundless; there's no effort involved. Let's say I float. I float through the other rooms in the house, to find what I already know is there. Olympios, gnawing roast meat from a plate piled high with bones, grease running down his chin, while Pretty plays with my empty jewellery box.

Ambracis and Agapios's slave are in my room, Ambracis on her knees before him; I have to spy over Philo's shoulder to see them. Philo is fisting himself faster than he's ever done anything in his life.

I'm in the courtyard dying when the house explodes with the sound of their voices, from all corners, all shouting at the same time. Singing? I don't know what it's called. They all arrive together. A cloud of startled birds poofs up from a tree; somewhere the dog, no longer a puppy, starts to howl. A crack runs up one wall from floor to roof; I watch the black line of it tracing like a raindrop running upwards. High, high up, a line of dry lightning silently continues the rent. I close my eyes.

*Daughter.*

I open my eyes and see Tycho in the corner of the courtyard. He squats, wrapped in his great filthy horse-blanket, rocking and mumbling to himself. Has he been here all this time?

"Tycho." I go to him, put my hand on his shoulder. "Tycho, your lady is here."

He looks at me with unseeing eyes.

"Tycho." I touch his forehead, his cheek. I try to get him to stand, but he won't. "Tycho!"

He rocks, mumbles.

"Are you hungry?"

Nothing.

In the kitchen I pick through the scraps and sort out a plate of stale bread and salt fish, and a cup of water from an almost empty jar. No way to know if it's fresh. I take it back outside and set it in front of him. "Are you cold?"

He shoves it all away, so abruptly that the cup spills and the fish flips into the dirt.

I understand the goddess is punishing the house. I understand it's because of me. She is visiting her feelings upon my house: jealousy, hurt, abandonment, betrayal. All I had to do was love her.

I decide to go looking for mercy, for Tycho if for no one else. A reprieve, or a few days' rest; any crumb. At the garrison, I'm shown straight to Thaulos's quarters. He looks happy to see me.

"There!" he says. "I knew you'd solve it. Clever father, clever daughter. How was your service?"

I say, "My service?"

"At the temple."

I tell him I've left the temple.

"Profitable, though, eh? You don't have to pretend. My wife serves there. I know how it works."

"Your wife," I say.

"The army's on the move, coming home, you'll be happy to know."

I nod.

"Soon you'll be having babies. Little babies running all over, and all this unpleasantness will be forgotten. What a gift to your husband, the house all settled! You should feel proud."

I close my eyes and see Thale. I open my eyes.

"It *is* all settled?"

I close my eyes and see Simon's rhubarb. I open my eyes.

Exasperated: "But then why did you go to the temple?"

I shake my head.

"Why have you come here?"

I tell him my servants are possessed.

Thaulos laughs, incredulous. "You've brought me absolutely nothing?"

Nothing.

⚬❀⚬

Tycho looks up when I enter the courtyard and says, "Lady," as though he is lucid. I ignore him and go to my room. Tricks of the goddess. Fortunately Ambracis and Agapios's slave are gone. Warm clothes, the bracelet I hid under a loose stone in the courtyard. In the kitchen I'm at a loss. Water? A knife? I turn around and Tycho is there, a bear in the doorway. "Lady."

I push past him, back through the courtyard to the stables. But the horses are gone. Sold, I guess.

"Lady."

I'll sell the bracelet in the market, buy a day's food, walk at night, hide during the day. If I make it to Athens, Theophrastos will have to take me in. He'll have to.

"Lady." Tycho plants himself between me and the gate. "You must do as your father would expect of you."

"I'm going to Athens."

I see the goddess return; I see the sudden flare in his eyes. He kneels abruptly, like he's been struck on the back of the head. "No," he says.

*No*, she says.

"It hurts," he says.

I ask him where.

He turns his wide, crazy eyes to mine.

"You have my leave to eat," I tell him. "And drink, and light a fire. You have my leave."

"Not Athens," he says.

*Not Athens.*

I ask her, *Where then?*

"Think of your father," the goddess says through Tycho. Tycho's mouth and voice. "What has your father left you?"

*Books. Knowledge.* What, indeed?

When I come back from the butterfly room—vaginal dilator in hand—he's in the corner of the courtyard again, rocking and mumbling.

✺

Well, what would *you* think if you saw me? Hurrying through the streets alone—morning still, the sky soft and white with cold—carrying nothing but my father's implement. The men look bemused but the women know. They shrink back from it. They clench. My hair is long and loose behind me as I stride. They part for me. I feel a bit like the goddess herself, with my implement instead of a bow, then realize she'll punish me for such thoughts. Too late. I walk faster.

The route to Glycera's house is familiar now. The turn in the road, the particular quality of light in the air just by this building here. The smell of baking, then figs, always figs. Five narrow steps up and into a quieter street—posh, elegant. The widow's house is set back from the others, right at the end.

There's a man coming out of her gate: Euphranor. He stops when he sees me.

"Where's your guard?" he asks. I don't answer. He looks at the implement and his eyebrows go up and stay there. "Really?"

I tap on the gate.

"About your farm." He's got his head on the side, studying the implement. "I know I said I could make it profitable for you, but it's winter. There will be no money coming from it before next summer at the earliest. Meanwhile—"

I tap louder.

"It's winter," he says. "Cold at night in a tent at the garrison. I need my home."

"Take it."

"No, but listen—"

I whang the gate with the implement. Now there's a sound they can't ignore.

"I've had word from Thaulos," he says. "Terrible man. He told me what happened. I'm shocked, shocked at his assumptions. That you would even consider stealing from the goddess. Paying off your debt with votive offerings. Gods, it's blasphemy. Foul blasphemy, eh, Pythias?"

Why does no one come?

"We might share the house, you know." He touches my hand. "Pythias, stop. Listen. I like you."

Thale and the rhubarb and the smell of Myrmex's burning hair and Philo peeping and Ambracis slurping and Herpyllis looking at Pyrrhaios and Daddy looking at Herpyllis and I will never touch myself ever, ever again.

Euphranor's looking down at my hand, which he's holding, breathing like he's been running, only he hasn't.

I take my hand back and two-handedly whang the implement on the gate again. The big slave finally comes.

"You're magnificent," Euphranor says. "I've always wondered how those work."

The slave closes the gate behind me.

"Think about it," Euphranor says.

I have already thought.

❦

Glycera receives me in a room I haven't seen before, a lush cave hung with furs and hot with braziers. Her hot room, her winter room. The cushions are red and gold. She rises from her couch to embrace me. I am not thinking not thinking not thinking about how her hair is all mashed down at the back.

I don't say hello. "Clea, the midwife. Where does she live? Where can I find her?"

The thing about Glycera is she's sincere. I read empathy in the way the shoulders drop, the head goes to one side, the eyebrows furrow in concern. Her eyes slip to the implement, now dangling from my hand to the floor, and her eyes flare in horror. "Child, oh child," she says.

But I am not in the mood for her perfumed bosom.

"There are alternatives," she says. "I know women in my position usually think otherwise. But I love babies, I love them. I'd help you with it. Ask my girls! I've never put one out because of a baby. Look at Meda. Didn't I do everything I could for Meda?"

I could nod.

"How far—?" She abandons the sentence to perform the calculation herself. She looks doubtful. "Before your father died?" she says. "Quite a while before?"

"What?"

"You're at least two moons, if you know for sure. Who was it? A student of your father's? Some boy in Athens? Well, it doesn't matter. As I say, no one understands better than me the kind of troubles a young girl can face. You were right to come to me."

"I haven't come to you."

"Shall we put that awful thing away?" She seems not to have heard me. She calls for a slave and points at the implement.

I hug it to my chest. "Clea," I say. "I just want to find Clea."

"I don't understand."

"I'm not pregnant." She winces at the term, as Gaiane and her mother did so long ago. "I didn't come here to stay. Please. If you won't tell me, I'll have to find her some other way."

She stands. "Who, then?"

I don't think you can get pregnant eating it, but who knows. The lie is easier. "Ambracis. One of my slaves."

"You treat them well."

"She has no worth if she dies."

Glycera blinks, then tells me, "Clea lives in the old town, behind the market. I'll send my slave with you. Really, you shouldn't be walking out alone. Where's your man?"

"Just at the bottom of the hill. I told him to wait there."

"Why?"

I adjust my woollens around me and get a better grip on my implement. "He was getting on my nerves."

Glycera leads me out through a different door than the one I came in, into a room that is a smaller version of her luxurious cave. Small, dark, warm, all furs and cushions. "Look who's come to see us," Glycera says.

This windowless room is darker than the first, and it takes my eyes a moment to make out Meda. It takes me a moment longer to make sense of what I'm seeing: she's nursing an infant. She smiles at me, then the baby, then back at me. The baby's eyes are closed, though it's still sucking. She smiles at Glycera, who puts a finger to her lips and leads me out.

"The baby son of a local merchant." Glycera pats my shoulder. "She's working as a wet nurse while she recovers. Recovers in her body and in her mind. Usually she works at their house, but occasionally she brings him back here. It's the best thing that could have happened, really. Did you see her face just now?"

Before I can stop myself, I say, "That's horrible."

Glycera's smile sweetens further. "You're very young, aren't you? Running your own house, delivering babies, serving the goddess, knowing what's best for everyone. Not needing any-one's help. You're really extraordinary."

"No."

"Milk should never be wasted." She looks again at the imple-ment. "You'll mutilate her with that. Maybe you don't care. Just a slave, eh? You've never had one of those up you, have you?"

"No."

"It's not for us to pick and choose the blessings of the gods. Milk is a gift. To the baby, to Meda, and to my household, which benefits from the money she brings in. I really don't care what you think of us. Follow this road straight to the market, then go up the weavers' alley. She's the seventh door on the right."

I thank her.

"Good luck," she says. "For your girl's sake. I'm sure *you'll* be just fine."

✿

Just at the bottom of the hill is Tycho: my lie to the widow made manifest. The goddess put him on her palm and blew him here, like chaff. How else?

"Lady," he says, "Lady." He's wringing his hands, shifting from foot to foot like he has to pee. "There's a man at the house. He says he lives there."

"Yes." I start walking the straight road to the market, as the widow directed. Tycho follows. "His name is Euphranor. The house belongs to him."

"Lady," he says. Surely it's the goddess sparking in him, her spirit inhabiting his body, moving him along like a puppet. I left him past sight and speech; how else is he so quickly recovered? "Lady, he walked right in the front gate, calling for you. Laughing."

"That's not possible. I just talked to him. He was just here. How can he be in two places at once?"

We walk together for a while, not talking. I feel ragged with confusion.

"I'm sorry," I say finally. "I'm sorry I left you."

"Lady," the goddess says.

"You were kind to me. You took care of me. You deserved better from me." The goddess looks confused. "Release me from your service." Now the goddess looks afraid. "I know I still owe you a debt, and I'll find a way to pay. I will. But you have to release me."

"Lady, you're ill," the goddess says.

Odd how she can so completely resemble Tycho, with his mud-brown eyes and soldier's stubbled head, the great bulk of him, even his leathery smell. My father, in me, begins to wonder about the mechanics of divine possession. Perhaps Tycho acts as a kind of filter or shell, and something of him remains even as the goddess shines through the cracks and pinholes. Perhaps Tycho's still here, somehow—confused, terrified, but here. Perhaps I need to speak *to* Tycho rather than around him; perhaps the goddess is not as free as I thought.

I set the implement down at my feet and take both his hands in both of mine. "I free you, Tycho," I say. This is as public a declaration as any; market-goers flow around us like water, looking openly, crooked-smiling. "I free you, Tycho, from service to my father's house, as a reward for your loyalty to him and to me."

*Release me, Lady.*

"Lady, no." Tycho shakes his head, like I'm three again. "Your father required me to serve you until your marriage. I obey your father."

I let his hands go. "I free you!" I say loudly. Around me, people are laughing.

"Lady." Tycho picks up the implement for me. "You can't free me. A girl can't."

I snatch the implement back and run. I lose him quickly enough in the crowd, and then there's the seventh door, which opens for me just as I'm raising my fist.

✹

Clea sets me to memorizing aphrodisiacs. Not the hocus-pocus of Herpyllis's world—the iunx spells and burnt offerings and midnight mutterings—so much as the kind of science that would have pleased Daddy. Mostly, Clea explains, we prescribe seediness: quince, sesame, pomegranate. Olive oil for lubricant, honey for sweetness. I must look stupid because she says, "Not off a spoon."

I'm sent into the back room when she meets with clients, mostly well-to-do women trying to conceive, or woo back wayward husbands; sometimes young bridegrooms who can't persuade their wives to—

I listen at the door. Clea is patient, serious, respectful, never lewd. *Perhaps*, Clea says, and *Have you considered?* The clients tell her everything, quicker than I would ever have guessed. *She only likes it this way, he wants me to put my finger up there, she says it hurts, he always cries after.* They pay nicely for Clea's advice, and we sell oils and creams and other things. After, sometimes, she'll raise her eyebrows at me, knowing I've had my ear to the door. She says there's nothing she hasn't heard at least two or three times a week for most of her adult life.

She explains the business to me the night I arrive. Not sex, but the before and after: aphrodisiacs and midwifery, contraception and abortion. She is as two-faced as her work. Quiet and modest with her clients; frank and easy with her friends, the others with whom she shares her house. In the evening, they drift in: three more midwives, plus a couple of men who have no clear occupations—assistants, security, companions—it's all fluid. They sit around the big room late into every night, eating and drinking and laughing and singing and telling stories. I understand they have no family but each other. They are dregs who have drifted to the bottom and settled together.

"Who's this?" one of the men asks the first night. His name is Candaules. A pair of hunting dogs nip at his heels and he carries a new-born puppy, whose head he knuckles while it blinks blissfully.

"This is Pythias," Clea says. "She's with me."

"I thought I was with you," Candaules says.

Clea takes the puppy from his arms and kisses its face and hands it back to him with a smile. "There's lots of Clea to go around."

That first night I keep to the corners, cooking and tidying and playing with the dogs and puppies. There are always puppies underfoot, play-fighting or looking for a cuddle, reminding me of Nico. The big room is high-ceilinged and dark, smoky from the brazier in the middle of the floor, around which they lay their sleeping mats. They drink themselves to sleep. They smoke, too, from a pipe that makes them happy. One of the men whittles phalluses, life-size and a little bigger; Clea explains we sell those, too. We sleep all about on the floor around the brazier, much like puppies ourselves, under mounds of blankets in the warm puppy-smelling dark. Their voices continue even after the fire is down to embers.

I learn the language of sex, a language hidden in plain sight: *tumbling chariots, visiting the sausage-seller, the double scull, the smelter, the trireme, the lioness on a cheese grater.* They laugh and laugh. They kiss and sigh and cry out. I sleep between Clea and wall, facing the wall while she services Candaules, who favours the *wicker basket on horseback,* and later another midwife, who shares with Clea *a sparrow's breakfast.*

"No one will touch you," she whispers over her shoulder, sensing my sleeplessness, deep in the night. "I told them you were mutilated, and in great pain."

"Thank you," I whisper.

੨◎੩

*I can't have another,* I hear, more than once a day. *It'll kill me. It's too soon. It's too late. I'm exhausted. Give me something. There must be something.*

There's always something. Cheesecloth, if he doesn't mind. A douche, after. Counting the days. Clea teaches them the safe days and they nod, doubtfully. They're desperate; nothing feels safe. If it's already begun, there are teas for sale. Sometimes they'll lie down on the table and Clea will have a look, feel around, and ask me to fetch a tool she has that's smaller than my implement. There's crying then, pain and blood, and afterwards a good deep sleep while we change the laundry and prepare a child's meal of warm milk and sweet bread for the woman. Clea instructs them how to explain it to the husband: a miscarriage brought on by exertion. She is to tell him she needs rest, much rest, and no relations for—

"How old is your youngest?" Clea will ask, and the woman will say, and Clea will tell her a number of moons, and say, "How does that sound?"

They will nod, weakly.

When the women are gone, Clea cleans her equipment.

❧

I go into private homes with her, to assist at births. I am calm and quiet and play up my Athenian accent; the grandmothers take to me. There are no live births. Each time, she sends me back to the house to tell one of the men she needs a puppy.

"Why?" I ask the first time.

"To be kind," Clea says. "We strangle the puppy and bury them together. That way, the baby won't be alone."

❧

I join them now in the evenings around the brazier with my cup of wine.

"I had a good one today," one of the women will begin.

They tell work stories, sad stories, bawdy stories, sex stories. The brazier crackles, the puppies sigh in their sleep, the wind rages outside. While they talk, I drift into myself. I hear and don't hear their tales of the prostitute who served an entire unit in one night and walked away after; the girl who pushed out four babies, one after another, like a cat's litter; the man who tallied his lays by notching his lintel every morning upon his return, until the morning it collapsed and killed him. I hear and don't hear their tales of the newest priestess of Aphrodite, the one who has to wear a veil in the temple so the goddess won't get jealous (good advertising, the midwives agree; no one has yet seen her face, though people flock to the temple now to catch a glimpse of her; probably quite plain, though with a graceful walk; the midwives have been to see for themselves); the preternaturally beautiful baby born to Achilleus the architect's wife, who tells anyone who will listen that the pleasure of his conception was so extreme that she suspects divine interference (Achilleus the architect will nod, apparently pacifically, during these confessions, as though modestly conceding that yes, yes, it's possible he was possessed by a divine sexual fire, after all look at the infant, that hair, that skin, those eyes!, and what if he himself is a short stout bald worrying man whose wife is taller and louder than he is, what if?); the man the midwives themselves pay to cock around town, putting it wherever he can to keep them all in business.

"Really?" I say. I haven't heard about him before.

They start; they thought I was drunk, or sleeping, or in the easy shadowland between drink and sleep.

"You pay someone?" I prompt, because they're staring at me, silently.

One of the men touches the knife on his belt with one finger.

"Let's sing," I say. I hold my cup up high. "A hymn to the goddess. More wine to honour the goddess!"

"Stop it, Pythias." Clea leans back against her latest companion. "You're a bad actor. You're not drunk. You heard something you shouldn't, eh? Usually you know to keep your mouth shut."

There's a movement in the shadows behind me. Clea's a bad actor, too, with her show of relaxation.

"I don't know what I heard," I say. "I don't think I actually heard anything."

"Actually," Clea says.

The one behind me moves closer. I hear his breath. I say, "After, will Candaules kill a puppy to go below with me?"

Clea glances over my head; an understanding through glances; the one behind me withdraws, a little. After a moment of nothing, I hear the knife being sheathed.

"He came to us," Clea says. "New in town, offering his services. We laughed him off, at first. We laughed him off for nine months, until the first jump in births—we had more work than we could handle. Then he came to us again and said he'd given us nine months for free, but if we didn't start to pay him, he'd move on to another town."

"How long ago was this?"

"Five years. It's gotten so we can spot which are his. There's always something not quite right. Not quite natural. It's not just the baby not looking like the husband, though it's that, too. Though the parents don't seem to notice it; they're in a kind of daze. Sometimes the babies are deformed, sometimes too perfect. And the women all seem—dulled down, sort of. Like they can't properly remember their lives before."

I think of Meda.

"You know the health of the baby is determined by the quality of the act of conception," Clea says. "Vigorous act, vigorous baby. Unwilling act, colicky baby. I've often wondered about the ones that are his."

"Achilleus the architect's wife," I say. "But then what about the deformed ones?"

Clea nods. "We told him at the outset, the women had to be willing. I wasn't going to pay him to rape. We followed him for a few nights, too, just to be sure."

"And you were sure?"

"Oh, yes." Clea nods, shakes her head; smiles despite herself, remembering. "*Ai.* I think maybe it's that he works too hard, sometimes, and the quality of his seed suffers. That's why some of the children—well. It's not the babies he cares about, though. They're just the side effect, the by-product. It's— I don't know how to explain."

"It's the women," I say.

"It's the seduction, certainly. The hunt." Clea shakes her head. "That's not it either, though, entirely. There's something very sad about him at times."

The others nod, murmuring.

"It's more like a hunger." Clea taps her finger to her lips. "A sickness, maybe. He can't stop. He couldn't, anyway, and it suited us well enough when he couldn't. And now, all of a sudden—"

"Maybe he just needs a rest."

"That one? He'll rest in his grave."

"Does he want more money?"

Clea shakes her head. "We offered him everything we could think of."

The fire flares up, spitting sparks onto the floor; the shape behind me steps forward to tamp them out. He looks at me apologetically, shrugs; it's Candaules. He sits back in his place.

"We think he's pining," Clea says. "That he's fallen in love with some little scrap of a flat-chested thing somewhere who won't have him, and now he doesn't know what to do with himself. We'd pay *her*, if we could find her."

"What does he look like?"

They've relaxed now; they're pouring more wine, feeding the fire, whispering to each other. They're still keeping an eye on me, though. What do they think I'm going to do?

"We can't seem to agree on that," Clea says. "We think he's a bit of a shape-shifter."

"Handsome?"

"Some days." Clea holds up the wine; I shake my head. She pours for herself. "Sometimes I think he makes himself dull so he can go unnoticed. To be able to slip in and out of places without anyone looking at him twice. And then sometimes of course he's a right peacock."

"Wait, though." I sit up straight, trying to understand. "Once he's gone, surely there'll still be babies born. You seriously think this one man services the entire town? Won't people like Achilleus the architect and his wife just go back to having uglier babies?"

"We thought so too, at first," Clea says. "At first. But haven't you noticed? They're all unhealthy now. We think he's punishing . . . everyone, really. The mothers, the babies, the families, us."

I shake my head. The room is quiet again.

"Since you came to town, come to think of it. What do you make of that?"

I shake my head. "I haven't met a man like that. No one's approached me that way. Well, except—"

"Except?" Clea says.

I shake my head.

"Except," Clea says.

"There's a cavalry officer."

The room is dirty, rough, sour with wine and dogs and lust. Clea's friends listen wide-eyed as children who know the story to come and need to hear it again anyway.

"That's the one," Clea says. "We think he might be a god."

*Tick, tick, tick*, the tiles fall into place like in that game Daddy used to play with Herpyllis in the courtyard, late into summer evenings.

"If you're the one he wants, who are we to deny him?" Clea says. "He'll reward us for bringing you to him."

"Gods don't behave that way," I say. "My father taught me that. God is far, far away. Not a man or a woman. More like a force."

They're listening.

"A beautiful vase," I say. "Think of a beautiful vase. Its beauty might prompt a man to buy it. That's its force. But the vase itself is oblivious. That's like god."

"What are you talking about?" Clea says.

"My father," I say. I'm trying to remember the exact words, and the sound of his voice. "My father said people lean back into the idea of benevolent gods to avoid standing on their own two feet. People lean back into each other in the same way. It's not real."

"That's a small, cold world your father lived in."

I say nothing.

"Do you live there, too?"

"I don't know," I say.

I don't have many things here, not much to collect: a change of underclothes Clea gave me when I arrived, and the implement.

"You'll bring him to us," she says, watching my tiny packing. "Or we'll find you, and we'll give you to him."

At the door, she presses her cheeks to mine and then pushes me out into the starry cold.

❧

I wake in pain, cold and awfully cramped, in the hollow of a tree not far from the east side of the channel, in the shadow of the garrison on the hill just across the water. It was deep night when I left Clea's, black and raw cold, and my instinct had been to curl up somewhere and die on my own terms. But a knife at my throat to make more babies for the midwives to save, or not—no. I started to walk, in case they should find me in a nearby alley at dawn and change their minds.

I heard sloppy singing as I walked, and shouting, and once the shriek of a woman's laughter from an upstairs window. *Really?* I thought. *Really?* Was the world really as lewd and drunken and dangerous at night as in stories? Wasn't that a bit ridiculous? Didn't the rapists and murderers have to sleep, too? I kept moving, kept to the shadows. I kept a firm hold of the implement and walked away from any light or sound, any life. At the channel, I realized I was a prisoner in Euboia; at least until dawn, when the ferryman would come. I stood for as long as I could—Daddy had taught me the danger, the siren call of warm sleep in cold—then squatted, and finally let myself doze sitting up as the first pink wine spilled low across the sky. Pretty, brainless dawn. I hugged the implement like a puppy inside my woollens, and rested my head against the tree trunk.

I hear the ferryman's bird-like call and the *plash* of his pole. I stand and beat the pins and needles from my legs with my fists, then limp down the bank. He takes the coin I hold out. I clomp onto the raft, feet still prickling from my awkward spell beneath the tree, and sit down.

"What's that?" He unties us casually, automatically, coiling the rope while looking curiously at the implement, which I've laid across my lap. Daddy taught me to see actions learned by the body, actions so habitual the body could work without the brain. To be good at anything physical, he taught me, you had to reach that point. That was a way to judge people, too, work-men and slaves, how easily they moved in their bodies. That told you of their experience, more than words could.

"It's a dilator." My tongue refuses *vaginal*. I am a lady, still, barely. "It's for babies."

"Eh—it's not." The current is quiet; I wonder if we're almost at the change of the tide. He sets the paddle down and reaches for a pole. "I had five myself. I never saw one of those."

"Maybe your wife did."

"What wife?" His face cracks open in a delighted smile; I've fallen for whatever he wanted me to. "Five babies, five different girls." He stops in the middle of the channel, pole planted in the depths. "I've seen you before."

I'm too tired to lie. "Yes."

"You shouldn't be alone."

I don't answer.

"Tell you what." He fishes my coin from inside his clothes and holds it out. "You keep this."

I take the coin but don't put it away. If he's hoping to see where I keep my pouch, he's out of luck. He starts poling again and we crunch against the opposite shore in a few heartbeats. With the same thoughtless ease, he loops the rope around the large rock he uses for his Western cleat.

"Thank you, Charon," I say.

He shakes his head. "I've heard that joke before." He takes an unsteady, lurching step toward me, as though thrown off-balance by the bobbing raft, and kisses my mouth. I jerk back. His taste is sour, rotten. Bad wine, bad teeth. His face cracks again.

"Thank you, Grandfather," I say.

For a moment neither of us moves. Then I'm halfway up the slope and he's calling after me, *Wait, wait. Your baby-thing.*

I don't stop. There's payment, if you like: a kiss, a handful of wool where he'd hoped a bigger breast would be, and a vaginal dilator. *For you; enjoy.*

⁂

The neighbourhood, around the backside of the hill topped by the garrison, is only a short walk away now. The streets are quiet; it's early still. Lately it's always early, or late. I'm aware of my own evil smell, lank hair, damp dirty clothes, throbbing head. Fatigue has scrubbed the inside of me raw, like a handful of sand. I don't recognize the house at first and am unsurprised; the gods have plucked and replanted the neighbourhood, perhaps, or I'm addled—punch-drunk from the effort of continuing, these past few weeks. Mere weeks, only, still. I walk to the end of the street where we used to live, then back again, ticking the houses off against the map in my mind. I recognize this one, with the painted lintel; and the next, with the chickens in the yard; and the next, with the pretty gardens and the sundial; and the next, the one next to ours, with the big cypress. Our house—mine, Euphranor's, someone's—is now overgrown with vine leaves, but after a moment of staring I recognize familiar details: gate, plant pots, trees, the diagonal crack in the stone walkway.

Vines don't grow in winter.

I stand still, cautiously putting this thought together.

"Lady."

Behind me. Sitting in the street in his filthy horse blanket, a greasy cloth wound around his stubbled head. He struggles to stand. I go to him and search his face. His eyes are clear. The joy of this stabs me unexpectedly deep. "Tycho."

"Lady."

I want to touch him. It's the oddest thing.

"I've been waiting for you," he says.

"I know."

He studies my chin. "Euphranor is master of the house now."

I nod.

"He's inside."

"Yes."

We both look at the house.

"Vines don't grow in winter," I say. Like a test.

"We can't cut them down," Tycho says. "Blades can't cut them."

"It's Dionysus, isn't it. Euphranor is Dionysus."

Tycho's eyes skip over me, hair clothes feet, not settling anywhere for long. Taking my measure. He looks back at the house. "He's been looking for my lady."

"Is he—"

Tycho lets his eyes touch mine, so briefly. "No," he says. "He's brought order back to the house. It's clean and tidy and we obey him. He treats us well. He's kind. He's been building up the storeroom, as well as he can this time of year. He only insists on order, cleanliness and tidiness. That and looking for you. He sends one or other of us out every day into the city, searching."

Here, in the cold street with Tycho, these feel like my last moments of—what? The end of one life and the beginning of another. Lesser; another lesser life. That's what I fear. That's what keeps me out here, in the cold. Yet less than what? Did I have so much without knowing it? What did I have before that I don't have now, that I could possibly recover in this world? Charon, indeed.

"There's something else." Tycho runs a hand over his stubble in that familiar gesture. "Someone else, another one. He comes every day. He comes to the gate and asks for you."

A sound from inside the courtyard: horse's hooves, a whinny, the clinking of tack. Someone is coming.

"Here." Tycho leads me a little way down the street, out of sight of the gate. We step back into some trees and watch until the gate has opened and closed and Euphranor has ridden past on his big black animal, not seeing us. Heading for the garrison. Handsome, today.

"A strange young man," Tycho continues. "Every day for a week now he's been coming, asking for you. He runs, though, if he gets the least smell of the master."

"Strange how?"

"Familiar." Tycho touches his stubble, his temples, covers his eyes, uncovers them, looks at me. "Lady?"

The glaze has returned.

"You should go in now," I say, though it hurts me.

"I have to wait for my lady."

"Yes." I take from his hands the greasy cloth he used to cover his head against the cold. It's big enough to cover me. "You should wait just inside the courtyard, there. Then they can bring your breakfast."

He looks confused.

"Just inside the gate." I give him a little push. "Then you can see the street and inside the house, too. It's the best spot. Your lady wants you to wait there."

He goes in. I go too, not far; back to the spot in the trees where we watched Euphranor pass. I wrap the greasy cloth all around me, covering my body and my hair and most of my face, and squat like a beggar in case anyone should notice me.

I spend the day in sleep's shallows, waking with a start at any sound or movement: the neighbours' comings and goings, birdsong, peddlers with their rattling carts, calling out new milk and bread and fish and trinkets and remedies and firewood and water. I buy a drink and a cake from a man who, when

I touch my throat to fake muteness, takes me for a boy. *Here, lad*, he says, and gives me my right change. Each time I think I can't sleep anymore, I'm off again, drifting, until the day's gone and it's dusk.

The street is busier now than it's been all day: people returning home, the night vendors making their supper rounds, soldiers coming down off the hill for an evening in town. I watch a beggar approach our gate, a dirty, bearded boy with a bad limp. He doesn't knock, but peers in like he's trying to stick his head through the bars. After a few moments he steps back. The gate opens minimally, then shuts with a clang. Now the beggar has a heel of bread.

He turns in my direction and I see it's Myrmex.

He passes me, close enough for me to see the limp is real, and I follow him down the hill and toward the ferry. But he turns left, along the shoreline to the beach where I took Daddy to swim in his last weeks. Down, down, down the long dunes tipped with shadows, and back into the trees, into a deep tangle where he must sleep. He could have looked back anytime and seen me; he didn't. Coming closer, I see him bending over something on the ground, working at some-thing: a fire. I don't hesitate. When he hears the first stick crack under my foot, he jumps up and back, awkwardly, and I walk straight up to his astonished self and push him so hard he falls backwards. Down on his back and I keep coming, beating at his head and shoulders with fists, hurting him. He tries to bat my hands away from his nose and eyes, but doesn't otherwise fight back. When I stop, he's bleeding from his nose and lip, and crying a little, too.

I sit on a log and watch while he builds the fire into something usable. The light's going fast now. By the time he's done, I can't see the tears or the blood.

"Pytho," he says. Of course his voice plucks me like a lyre string.

He has a number of little packets of things, it turns out: kindling, dry clothes, dried fish, a leather roll of tiny knives I recognize as Daddy's. He worries through all these packets, looking for something with an anxious fussiness I hadn't known in him before. I accept some nuts and dried fruit without letting his hand touch mine. We sit across the fire from each other, warily eating.

"You're dirty," he says, after a while.

"You smell like pee and onions. What happened to your foot?"

He shakes his head.

"Fine," I say, and then we're not talking, again.

We finish eating and stare into the fire. After a while, he gets up and rummages around and throws a blanket at me. It hits me in the head. I wrap it around my shoulders. He sits shivering and I don't care. I'm glad.

"How's Nico?" he says finally.

"He went to Athens, to Theophrastos."

"That's good," Myrmex says. "He'll be safe there."

"Herpyllis went to Stageira," I say, when he doesn't ask. He grunts. "What happened to your foot?"

"A man put it on a chopping block. I thought he was going to cut it off with his axe, but instead he used the butt end on my ankle. I don't think it's going to heal."

The stars are out. The fire seethes, sounding like Herpyllis sucking her teeth in annoyance.

"I'm sorry, Pytho," he says. "I'm so sorry."

Let it come.

"I thought I could help, if it means anything," he says. "I took it to gamble, the money. I thought I could make more than enough for—"

*Our wedding*, I think. I can't stop myself. Of course that wasn't what he was going to say, but my mind makes it anyway.

"They were going to send me home," he says. "I wasn't going back there. I was going to make enough so we could choose for ourselves, both of us."

"Choose what?" I say softly.

He looks at me across the fire, utterly clear, utterly bleak. "Not that, little Pytho," he says. Again: "I'm sorry."

"You could have asked me. I would have given it to you. I would have given you everything. You didn't have to leave. You could have just asked."

He shrugs; such disinterest, now that suddenly I'm enraged. He doesn't get to choose when *my* life is over.

"Here." I hike my dress up to my thigh, rip off the pouch I have strapped there, and throw it at him across the fire. He catches it reflexively. "That's my last. That's everything I have. It's yours now. You understand?"

He's interested now. I can see he wants to look inside, to see how much is there. Instead he says, "I'm surprised Euphranor lets you carry money."

"*Euphranor?*"

He looks confused; caught.

"You think I'm living in that house with Euphranor?"

"Where else?"

I stand up. The dress falls back down over my legs; the blanket falls from my back. "Look at me. *Look* at me. Do I look to you like I've been living in a house with a man?"

He looks. I think he looks at me properly for the first time in his life.

"Come here," he says.

"Fuck you."

"Come here. I don't want this." He holds out my pouch.

When I reach for it, he grabs my wrist, and we go where we've been heading since the day he arrived: hello and goodbye in the same breath. After, he wraps us both in the blanket and holds me until I fall asleep.

When I wake, he's gone for good, with the money I carried in the pouch on my thigh, my last.

Kick, Pytho, kick.

I can't.

You can. Daddy won't let go. Kick, Pytho.

*Pytho kicks. Pytho can see the bottom, the hot fine dry sand she plays in on shore now swirling, liberated by the water. Water isn't blue when you splash it or pour it from your hands, but it looks blue when you look at the whole big sea. That's interesting.*

Kick, sweet.

*Pytho kicks, straining to keep her chin up. Daddy holds her hands, pulling her forward while he walks backward. He's letting his grip go softer and softer and Pytho knows he's getting ready to let go and make her do it by her own self. She crab-claws his hands with hers so he can't.*

Now put your face down.

*That Pytho can do. She puts her face into the water, eyes wide open, and holds Daddy's hands and kicks. She makes big splashes and wriggles her body and does silly-swimming.*

Good, *Daddy says when she stands up to catch her breath.* My little fishy. You're a good swimmer.

I know, *Pytho says.*

*Pytho is naked. Mummy's Herpyllis is up on the beach with the picnic and the baby. Herpyllis doesn't see why Pytho needs to learn to swim, but she isn't Pytho's mummy and she doesn't decide. Daddy and Pytho decide. Mummy is down below, but Pytho will be down below one day too, so that's all right for now. Meanwhile she's nice to Herpyllis, because Herpyllis belonged to Mummy when she was alive and Mummy was nice to her. Pytho waves and Herpyllis waves back with the hand not holding the baby. Pytho decides she will give Herpyllis a present.*

Look at me! *she calls, and puts her arms over her head and dives into the water and kicks kicks kicks, all by her own self, until she comes up coughing. Daddy is right there and scoops her out of the water and holds her up to the sun, his pet fishy, and she can hear Herpyllis clapping and others on the beach too, people they don't even know, and Daddy is hugging her and telling her she's brave and strong and she did it all by herself.*

Again, *Pytho says.*

*Again and again, all that afternoon, until she can swim even where her feet don't reach the sand, and Daddy never gets bored and leaves her, not even for a minute.*

"Hold still," Glycera says. "This is going to hurt."

She rips the wax from my eyebrow and I say a word.

"Don't be coarse," Glycera says. "Other one."

This time I'm silent, though my eye cries from the pain. Just the one eye. That's interesting.

"Much more effective than tweezing. The redness will fade in a few hours." She picks up my hand, looks at my fingernails, and makes a face. "They'll grow back, I suppose. Still. How did you let things go that far? I've never understood girls who don't care for their bodies. Men either, for that matter. My husband always let me take care of him that way. It's who I am, I suppose. You express your inside through your outside, no? Clean and tidy?"

"Yes, Mother." It's what I must call her now.

"You always were a ratty little thing," she says, but not meanly. "Never mind. Shall we talk about your hair?"

We talk about my hair, about how often I'll be expected to wash and comb it—more than I'm used to—and the styles that are appropriate for my age and station. Nothing too complicated, Glycera says; she wants me looking young. "Nothing perverse. Just your age, that's all. You don't need to try to look older than you are. I have older girls."

Meda enters the blue-sky room with a tray of jewels, and smiles her smile.

"How is the baby?" I ask.

Glycera nods, and Meda fetches him in his rush cradle. I ask if I might hold him. Glycera smiles at me like she's going to cry, and nods again at Meda, who lifts him gently and puts him in my arms. He doesn't wake. I kiss his hair and breathe his smell.

"One day," Glycera says, and smiles again at Meda, at me. The baby sighs in his sleep.

They spend a long time over the jewels, holding them up to my cheek to check the colours. Glycera calls for the other girls to solicit their opinions. She explains that each girl has a signature colour, to show her to best advantage.

"And to stop us fighting over clothes," Meda says. The other girls giggle. This is the longest sentence I've ever heard her say.

Meda is pale green. Obole is lilac; Aphrodisia is blue. Glycera herself is orange. Yellow, they agree, makes me look sallow. Shell pink appeals to them, but I reject shell pink. Dark green? Red is coarse. Grey is dull. Brown?

The girls sniff. They don't like brown. I touch a ring, gold, set with a piece of earthy agate.

"Brown could make her skin look lighter." Glycera holds the ring to my cheek. She fingers through the tray and finds another, darker. "What do you think, Pythias?"

It reminds me of cumin, and the colour when I close my eyes, just before sleep.

"Brown." Glycera turns the word over in her mouth, tasting it. "Unusual. Well. Unusual suits you, doesn't it?"

"Yes, Mother."

I take my lessons in the big dining room, which Glycera says they use for parties. At this time of year, it's cold. Glycera says the cold will force me to concentrate; something Daddy believed also. I have dance lessons and singing lessons and lessons in the art of conversation. These are with Glycera herself, who begins by offering some opinions about Alexander's military campaigns. She can talk about tactics, formations, terrain. I tell her Daddy once accompanied the king on campaign and saw him in all his glory. Daddy had gone along to serve with the medics, I explained, and because the king himself had asked him to.

"Good," Glycera says. "That's good. Very interesting. You can use that."

We talk about battlefield injuries and their treatment. We talk about medicine more generally. She quizzes me about my cycles, and finds out what I know about contraceptives: much, thanks to Clea. She wants to tell me about the act, but I tell her I've seen animals, and Daddy has explained most everything.

"All right," Glycera says. "Only you can't keep talking about your father. Once, at the beginning of a conversation, to remind the client of your bloodline. Then you must forget. The client wants to talk to *you*."

She asks me if I have particular interests, and says I'll speak most fluently about what I care about.

Do I have particular interests? Can I speak without Daddy speaking through me?

*Skeletons*, I think. "Poetry," I say finally.

"Yes, dear." She pats my hand. "Recitation is a lovely skill. In my experience, though, they don't want to listen. They want to talk." I must look disappointed because she adds, "Never mind. A dreamy young girl in love with poetry. That's very pretty. A very appealing type."

Now I am a type.

"Of course you're a type," she says. "We're each a type. And after a while you'll come to see that the clients are, too, and you'll learn to respond appropriately."

"What type are you?"

"Old." She's crisp, unoffended. "I'm Mother."

"And Meda?"

"No," Glycera says. "I'm not playing this game with you. You have to learn it for yourself. Now we're going to have an argument. Are you ready? They like a spirited argument, even a bit of cheek. Always with a smile."

We argue about the relative merits of empire and democracy; the Macedonian treatment of Athens; the virtues of friendship versus erotic love. I'm guessing there's a right side to this argument, but Glycera says not. We are *hetairai*, she says, worthy companions, not common prostitutes; we are not coarse. I remember not to mention Daddy, and at the end of the lesson she says I'm very good at conversation, a natural.

"Thanks," I say.

She shoots me a look. I wonder if I'll be reprimanded for my tone, but she says nothing.

She says she needs a lie-down, and tells Aphrodisia to show me cosmetics. We powder my face white and paint my eyes. "More, more," Glycera keeps saying from her couch across the room, waving a languid hand and not opening her eyes. "She's brown as a little nut." Aphrodisia's hands are tiny and she smells of roses. The powder makes me sneeze. She rubs a fingertip of oil on my lips, to soften the chap, and says I must do so every morning and night until they've healed. In the bronze, I look like I'm wearing a mask.

My coming-out party will be in ten days. Obole and Meda work on my dress, a tan gauze with darker brown embroidery. They want ties at the shoulder, but Glycera favours the more old-fashioned gold pins. Spikes. From these kinds of details, I'm putting together a picture of the type she thinks I am: brainy, fierce, Macedonian rather than Southern. A wild young Northern thing with a chest like a boy and a brain like a man. The embroidery pattern on my dress is all geometrics.

"No flowers?" I ask, and Glycera says no, no flowers. Aphrodisia is flowers; Obole is birds; Meda is herbs and green plants and seed pods; Glycera herself is fruits. Aphrodisia is sweet and simple and pretty; Obole is graceful and athletic; Meda is lovely and sad. My party is meant to introduce my type, and a bit of myself too: Glycera says we'll serve my favourite foods. What are my favourite foods?

"That's a lot of salt," she says, when I rattle off a list. "No sweets at all? Usually young girls like sweets."

I'm standing on a low table while they pin up my hem. "Sandals," Glycera says, considering. "Definitely sandals to the knee."

"Next you'll have me carrying a spear."

"Lippy." Glycera raises my chin with a finger, the way she does. "Have you ever been with a man?"

A question I've been waiting for. I was surprised she didn't ask within minutes of my creeping through her door and asking for sanctuary. "Three."

"All right, fine." Glycera shrugs. "I'm just trying to help. I'll give you some books to read, shall I?"

My salty, brown, spiky party is like the wedding party

I attended in Chalcis with Daddy: the same lulling golden warmth, the same rich ribboning scents of meat and wine, the same fine citizens in their finery, smiling fit to break their faces. At the last minute, Glycera decides not to powder me, and plucks all but a few pins from my hair, so it mostly hangs long and loose down my back. She almost sends me out barefoot, but decides that would be a touch too much. Her pet names for me have been evolving: now I am *orphan, waif, ragamuffin, scrap.* "Sweet little scrap," she says with her lip-biting, I'm-not-really-crying smile. "You remember the magistrate?"

I smile.

"Now, you see," Plios the magistrate says. "You've fallen on your feet, after all."

He's not the one I'm waiting for.

"Pythias." The priestess of Artemis puts her hand on my shoulder. "You have found a way."

She's not the one I'm waiting for.

He arrives late, after Glycera's speech, after the meal, after Aphrodisia has sung for me, and Obole has danced, and Meda has juggled two pears and a heavy earring, to much delighted applause. I haven't had to perform beyond a few words of thanks to the room. Glycera, in a final evolution, has turned to praising my wit. Soften them with pity and then quicken their interest; I see the scheme. We've moved to couches in the cave room. A slave announces him. Glycera leads him to the couch next to mine, and while she begins a general conversation on economics—a pre-set topic offering me opportunities to shine—he leans over and says quietly, "You're so angry, you're practically throwing sparks."

"I have a message for you. From Clea, the midwife. She wants to talk to you."

He waves a dismissive hand. "Boring."

"Mm."

He looks around the room. "What an awful party. Aren't you dying?"

"I'm dead. How's Tycho?"

"They're all fine. No fear, little Pythias. You know you can come see them any time."

I say nothing.

"You really think this is better than what I'm offering?" He means the room, the party, the guests, Glycera, my dress, all of it. "I'd take you swimming. Riding and swimming and hunting. I'd buy you books. What else?"

"My own spear?"

"Knives, spears, bows and arrows, a catapult."

I must smile because he does, too.

"Tell you what," he says. "I know how to get out of here. Together, single file, no looking back until we've reached the other side of the water."

"But who will lead and who will follow?"

He gets up and walks away. So that's how it would be.

Had he looked back, he'd have seen me moving to the magistrate's couch to challenge him—wittily—on a point of taxation.

∞◉∞

Plios the magistrate is not a bad man. He doesn't tell me I'm throwing sparks. He comes every afternoon as the sun is going down, between his work and his home. He greets Aphrodisia with a kiss when he sees her; I'm her replacement. He takes a warm drink in one of the big rooms with Glycera and me, chatting about his day. He likes to talk about his cases and solicit our opinions. I ask the kind of questions Daddy would have, about the practical day-to-day workings of the courts. Theory is one thing, Daddy always said, but practice another. If all you know is theory, you don't know anything.

"Well, take today, for example," Plios says on his third visit. "On paper, it was an open and shut case. The woman was accused of killing her husband with an iunx. There was plenty of evidence. They found the tablet with the curse, and the bird nailed to the wheel, and the ashes, and her maids confessed to helping her.

"Confessed," Glycera says lightly.

Plios stretches mightily, groaning with pleasure. "Glycera and I have this argument," he says to me. I'm sitting next to him on the couch, holding his hand. "She doesn't believe you can get an effective confession through torture."

"An eccentricity of mine," Glycera says. "What do you think, Pythias?"

"I agree." I turn his hand over in mine and massage the meat of his palm with my thumb, the way Glycera taught me. He sighs happily. "I've seen women in childbirth who would say anything, any lie, to make the pain stop. Why is she supposed to have wanted him dead?"

"The man's brothers say she had a lover. She wanted to marry this other man. He confessed, too." I switch to his other hand. "Open and shut when I read the brief. But in court—well."

Glycera signals to a slave, who steps forward with a tray of wine. She pours Plios a cup. He takes a sip and makes a face. "You've got mice," he tells Glycera.

I take the cup and smell it. Sour, faintly fecal. I signal to the slave, who steps forward again to remove the wine. Glycera looks mortified.

"Oh, it doesn't matter." Plios stands, pulling me up with him. "I don't need wine. My good Elene is expecting me for supper, anyway. She's told me, one more late night at work and she'll let the slaves prepare my meals from now on. I can't risk it. She's got a lovely light touch in the kitchen, my Elene. Lovely clear soups. After you, my dear."

I lead him to my brown room. He wants it sitting, with me kneeling between his legs, facing him. I still gag, but he doesn't mind. I've learned a bit of pain, a pinch or a scratch just before the peak, finishes him faster.

"Why was it different in court, though?"

We're wiping ourselves and dressing again. Three times, only, and already we have habits—I hold my hair up so he can repin the shoulders of my dress.

"Well, she was black and blue. She couldn't see out of one eye, it was so swollen, and she couldn't talk clearly because of her jaw."

"The brothers?" I straighten his clothes for him, his hair, rake smooth his beard with my fingers.

He shakes his head. "Everyone agreed they hadn't seen her since the death. She was taken in almost right away. That was the one thing everyone agreed on."

"Then I don't understand."

He looks at me with his clear, kind eyes. "It has to have been the husband."

"The one she killed?"

He nods.

"Did that change your decision?"

He looks at me a little longer, without answering.

I walk him to the gate. "I can't come tomorrow," he says. "But the day after, I can stay longer. Quite a bit longer."

I say, "All right."

It starts to rain. Big, reproachful drops.

"Gods." Plios laughs. "That was sudden. It's almost painful, isn't it? Well, go in. No sense both of us getting wet. I'll see you soon."

I kiss his cheek, as Glycera says I must, and go in, but not before the raindrops have stung the skin on my bare arms and shoulders. Hours later I'm freckled there with tiny red blisters, like burns from spitting oil.

The next day, I take the coins Glycera gave me to the temple and hand them over to the head priestess. Though I go veiled, accompanied by the big slave from Glycera's house, I feel the townspeople's eyes on me.

The next day is so stormy, the sun barely comes up. The sky is black all day and the rooms are like night. Plios stays for two lamps, a meal, and another lamp. The last time, I'm on my back when something makes me open my eyes. Past Plios's ear, I see a movement in the shadows where the wall meets the ceiling. As I watch, the colour curls back on itself and rolls in a single long peel down to the ground. Then the next wall, and the next.

When Plios notices, he's delighted. "We fucked the paint off the walls!"

After he's gone, I fix my hair and strip the bed. The paint curls crumble to dust when I touch them. I go to fetch the broom and dustpan and find Obole is ahead of me, trying to clean the big dining room. Every room in the house is afflicted. Glycera and Aphrodisia are on their knees, trying to scoop up the dust in their cupped hands.

"Is it the humidity?" Meda appears in the doorway, wrapped in a sheet. They all look at me.

"I'm not sure," I say. I think of Daddy, of Clea, of Euphranor, and add—honestly—"I doubt it."

✵

A client of Meda's, an importer named Karpos, hires us to adorn his house for an evening symposium. He's invited many prominent citizens of Chalcis. Glycera has taught me there are many kinds of intercourse between a man and a woman, and my sisters and I make our way through the room accordingly: stepping lightly on unsuspecting feet; pretending to trip and seizing elbows to steady ourselves; holding eye contact a little too long; taking a man's cup from his hand and sipping from where he sipped; occasionally licking our lips, to offer sightings of the tips of our tongues.

I glide into the courtyard. Karpos the importer made his money in wine, and the stonework is carved and painted with vine motifs. I scrape with my fingernail at a cluster of black grapes painted on a column.

"Here you are."

"Here I am."

"Hiding?"

I shrug.

"*I'm* hiding."

"I don't care."

"Course you care," Euphranor says. "Don't you want to know who I'm hiding from?"

I shrug.

"Everyone," he says. "Everyone but you."

I shrug.

"Do you want to see a trick?"

No.

"No," he says. "But I'm going to show you anyway."

He touches his finger to the painted column, where I've scored white scratches in the paint. The scratches heal.

"Very impressive," I say. "You can put paint back on as well as take it off."

"You noticed."

I turn to go back inside.

"I've been very kind to you," he says. "Very generous, very patient."

It comes then, the change. The grapes burst into reality from the paint on the columns, hanging plump and ripe from the marble; the air suddenly goes warm and druggy sweet; the god, behind me, flickers into himself like a flame catching a bit of paper. A slave passing through the courtyard sees this, hesitates, then runs into the house. As though a person could run from this.

"I'll kill Simon," the god says. "I'll kill Thale and Ambracis and Philo and Olympios. I'll throw the baby down the well.

I'll cut Tycho's throat in front of your face, so help me, Pythias. I'll make you watch."

I tell him Tycho's had enough.

"He's had enough when you decide he has," the god says. "It's entirely up to you."

Inside, I tell Glycera I have a client. I don't run; I walk.

✹⊙✺

The house is utterly overgrown with vines. It's early, still, and there's a supper laid out for us. Ambracis serves, eyes downcast, and Euphranor finds reason to summon each of the servants, one after another, on one pretext or another, so I can see they're all well, plus meek and obedient. The house is tidy and in good order; the disarray is utterly gone.

I tell him I won't do it in my father's room, and he says he understands.

I have the god in my old bedroom. I tell him what to do and he does it. I tell him what I want. It's not a matter of superior meltings or explosive joys.

"I love you," he says. Warm, naked, breathing hard. "I've loved you for so long."

I tell him he's not allowed to talk.

✹⊙✺

The next morning, I'm woken by shouting. I'm alone in the bed.

Tycho is blocking the gate, trying to keep someone out.

I wrap my fur tighter around my naked self and venture closer, barefoot.

A soldier. Filthy, haggard, knife drawn. His eyes are sunken in a way I know. His voice is deep and rough, with a bit of sandpaper in it.

"Then wake her," he's saying. "I'll wait." I step closer, and he sees me over Tycho's shoulder. "Pytho?"

I put my hand on Tycho's shoulder. *It's all right.*

"Cousin," I say.

His smile, so sweet it hurts.

III

Nicanor's ridden one horse and is leading a second. He smiles at me and sheathes his knife and dismounts and I open the gate and let him in.

"I went to Athens first," he says, looking around the courtyard. "You weren't there, but your brother was. And that tall fellow."

"Theophrastos," I say.

"He gave me all this money." He opens a saddlebag on the second horse to show me a small fortune in gold coin. "From your father's school. He said it rightfully belonged to me. Then I went to the garrison, here, and spoke to Thaulos. He said you'd be expecting me."

"Ah."

We both look down at the fur I've pulled tightly around me.

"I'd like a wash," he says. "And something to eat."

"Tycho," I say.

"Lady."

"Take care of our cousin. Give him whatever he wants."

"Will you put that lot in the storeroom?" Nicanor says to me, nodding at the saddlebags. "After you put some clothes on. You, Tycho. Lead on."

"Master," Tycho says. He's been playing his trick of keeping his big self half between us throughout this conversation.

"All right, man, I'm not going to eat her," Nicanor says. "Show me the kitchen while she sorts herself out. I want some eggs."

"This way, Master."

I lock up the bags and return to my room, where I put on the brown dress from last night. I find Nicanor in the kitchen breakfasting on bread dipped in a bowlful of raw egg. He eats standing. "Want some?"

I shake my head.

"Thaulos told me there's a man named Euphranor I owe some money to," Nicanor says, without looking at me. "Is that right?"

I nod.

"Does your family know? Herpyllis, or your brother?"

I shake my head.

"I've been on campaign for twelve years," he says. "I need rest. Your man here has explained the situation to me. It's all right, Pythias. I'm not going to tell your family. The townspeople will talk, I suppose, but that doesn't matter. I don't care. Stay home like you're supposed to, from now on, and you won't even have to see them. I'm not going to punish you."

He stops eating for a moment and looks at me to make sure I believe him.

"Oh," I say.

"Write to them," he says. "Your brother and the others. A small wedding, don't you think? Nothing too elaborate. How soon do you think they might come?"

"IS THAT WINE?" NICO ASKS. "No, not for me, I'll have water. Theophrastos has been teaching me. Water for thirst, wine for taste, that's what he says. I'm thirsty. Are these cups new? I don't recognize these cups. This is new." His cloak. "Do you like it? Theophrastos had it made for me. It's very good wool, very warm. It's almost too warm for this time of year. He's getting married too, did you know? You'll come to Athens for the wedding? I'm best in my class in astronomy and mathematics and I'm learning to play the *kithara* now. Theophrastos says I'm really good, especially considering I started so late. I brought it with me, I can show you. It's a really good one. Theophrastos says you become a better musician if you play on a better instrument. It was actually pretty expensive. I have my own room, it's bigger than my room here. You'll see when you come to visit me. You can come visit now, can't you? Now that it's spring and the army is home? Theophrastos says it's very safe for us Macedonians now. He says Daddy was over-cautious, but it's better to be safe than sorry. He says—"

My little brother breaks off mid-thought to launch himself into Herpyllis's lap and bury his face in her dress. She laughs and runs her fingers through his hair, slowly, over and over, until he lies still.

We're sitting in the courtyard, early evening, enjoying one of the first really warm days of spring: new green, new birds, heavy clothes and winter shoes abandoned for linen and sandals. Me, Nico, Herpyllis, Pyrrhaios, Nicanor. Theophrastos is in Daddy's old room, working. I think he wants to sit with us, but feels he'd be intruding on the family. Or maybe he feels he must keep Daddy's ghost quick. Pyrrhaios is family now; he and Herpyllis married in Stageira. He smiles often, touches her gently. And Nico—I can see he wants to love Pyrrhaios like a father. Nicanor sits on the far side of Pyrrhaios, listening with his head on one side to favour his good ear, patiently answering Pyrrhaios's questions. When no one is speaking to him, he withdraws into himself, sipping from his cup. He, too, is thirsty.

I spend a lot of time watching him. I am alert to him—his body, his moods, what focuses his attention and what releases it. I find myself wanting a private glance across the table, a casual touching of hands, any acknowledgement at all. But he is cool. His eyes don't change when he looks at me. He's tired, and spends a lot of time alone in the room he's chosen for himself. He dislikes loud noise. I've seen him wince at Nico's high spirits, less in dislike than in physical pain. He has a ringing in the good ear, he's told me, and he gets headaches. After we're married, I'll see if he'll let me put herb poultices on his temples, the way I used to do for Daddy. He's already told me he'll be keeping his own room.

Herpyllis asked after Myrmex within minutes of her arrival in Chalcis. I told her the truth: that he had stolen from us, that he was gone and he would not be coming back.

"I should be surprised," Herpyllis says. But her eyes still fill with tears.

"Who's Myrmex?" Nicanor asked.

"A poor relation. Daddy took him in years ago. He was like my brother."

"What did he steal?"

"Money." I hugged Herpyllis again. She couldn't stop kissing me, all over my face. "He was a little shit."

"*Pytho.*" Herpyllis looked mortified, then laughed. "Language!"

"He sounds like it," Nicanor said. "Good riddance, then. You'll excuse me."

Then he was gone to his room for the rest of the afternoon, leaving Herpyllis and me to supervise Pyrrhaios's unpacking, and generally boss him about. We laughed so much, the three of us, until Pyrrhaios looked at Herpyllis and said, "I don't care," and hugged me too, and I let him.

"We've missed you." He put his arm around Herpyllis and the two of them stared fondly at me. "We were so worried about you."

Love had wrought magic in him, a metamorphosis; he liked me now. Herpyllis was more relaxed than she'd been in the months before Daddy's death, and her prettiness was back, in her eyes, especially. They were happy together.

Now, in the courtyard, Pyrrhaios leans over to prise Nico off his mother's lap. "I can still pin you," he says, and takes a few steps away from the table, hauling Nico onto the ground to wrestle, to prove it. Nicanor flinches at Nico's delighted shrieks but, unusually, doesn't leave. He's making an extra effort tonight. The wedding is tomorrow.

Theophrastos appears in a doorway, drawn by the noise, and watches the wrestlers with his dry smile. Neither he nor Nicanor has Pyrrhaios's tree-branch arms. Pyrrhaios gives Nico the exhilaration of the body, Theophrastos that of the mind. What, if anything, will Nicanor give him? So far, they've barely spoken.

The next day's festivities begin at sundown. A priest comes to the house to supervise the ritual. Nicanor and I exchange gifts. He gives me a bolt of pink silk and a necklace set with pink tourmalines I'll wager anything Herpyllis picked out for him. I give him a branch of snow-white plum blossoms. I wanted to give him plums, for my first memory of him, but of course it's only spring. He holds the branch without curiosity, waiting to be told what to do next.

The wedding supper is hosted by Herpyllis and Pyrrhaios. Herpyllis explains each dish as it comes. *Beans with mint, you stew it with a ham hock, and honey bread, and lamb rubbed with spices, you have to crush them first and use quite a bit of salt, and quince cake of course, seedy quince cake!* A seedy meal for a seedy wedding night; I blush, and they beam.

Nicanor sits apart from me, and sips from his cup, and listens with his head cocked, smiling his polite, dull-eyed smile. Finally it's time for the procession back to the house. Normally we would walk from my father's house to my husband's; but here, of course, there's no distinction. This morning, I asked Nicanor if he wanted to stay in Chalcis, or return to Athens, or go somewhere else altogether. He looked at me and said, "I really don't care."

Nicanor takes my hand, and together we lead the wedding party, by torchlight, on a short walk up the street and back. In the few days she's been here, Herpyllis has taken the servants in hand and had the house scrubbed to a moony glow. Even the outside walls are clean and polished. At the threshold, Nicanor turns to thank the party. Then he leads me inside.

They have prepared Daddy's old bedroom, which is to be ours now.

We stand in the doorway. Many lamps are lit, and flower

petals toast in a brazier, scenting the room. The bed's laid with silk and fur, and there's wine on the table. Nicanor moves first; he goes for the wine. I attend to the brazier with the petals, blowing them out.

Nicanor glances over. "Thanks. Perfume makes me sneeze." He takes off his clothes and gets into the bed with his cup. "This wine is decent."

"It's a wedding gift. From Euphranor, I think."

Our first married conversation.

After a blank moment, he looks up at me. "You can read, if you like," he says. "The light won't bother me. You like to read?"

"There's no book here," I whisper.

He closes his eyes.

I take a lamp across the courtyard to Daddy's old work-room. The house isn't asleep yet. Doubtless they've noticed me; perhaps they'll think he's asked me to read to him.

When I return, Sappho under my arm, he's asleep.

After the first night, he leaves the big bedroom to me and returns to the small, windowless room he claimed as his when he first arrived. There's no sneaking, no pretence; he doesn't care who knows. Herpyllis takes me aside to ask if he's injured there.

"I don't know," I say. That hadn't occurred to me.

"But the first night—"

I shake my head.

"But then you aren't married."

"I suppose not."

"Pytho." She takes my shoulders in her hands so I have to look at her. "Do you want me to ask him?"

"No!"

"Then you have to find out. It's grounds for—"

I hold up my hand, *stop.*

"We can all see he's suffering," she says. "We all have compassion for him. But we have to think about *your* future, too."

"I said I'd do it."

"All right, all right, all right, I'll stop talking about it." But something else occurs to her. "It *is* him, not you? I know the first time can be—especially if you're shy, or—"

I close my eyes and stick my fingers in my ears.

"Forget I asked," Herpyllis says.

Nico comes loping into the kitchen, where we've been having our little talk, looking for another in an endless series of snacks. Herpyllis ruffles his hair, kisses me, and leaves us alone.

"You're so tall now," I say.

"Your voice is still deeper." He sits at the table and lets me serve him, bread and dried apricots. I sit down across from him. "I've missed you," I say.

"Me too." He eats an apricot. "Nicanor told me Daddy's will said he was responsible for me, and anytime I wanted to leave Theophrastos and come back to live with you, I could."

"Is that what you'd like?"

He looks at me steadily, with his clear, good eyes. "Not really," he says. "But I'll do it if you need me."

I lunge at him across the table, tackle him to the ground,

and tickle him until we're both breathless. "Who needs you?"
I say, again and again, digging my fingers into his armpits and
wiggling them. "Who needs you?"

That night, I go to Nicanor's room. I had thought to follow
him, very naturally, when he first went. Early, as usual; earlier
than the rest of the house. But courage failed me, and instead
I stayed up, playing tiles with Herpyllis and Pyrrhaios and
Nico, while Theophrastos read in his corner. We talked about
their respective journeys home, the day after tomorrow, and
Theophrastos's upcoming marriage, in the summer, when we
would all be reunited.

"And we'll come again, the moment you—as soon as you—
as soon as you need us." Herpyllis falters.

"She means when you get pregnant," Nico says. Daddy
taught us both not to be mealy-mouthed.

"That will be lovely," I say to Herpyllis. And to Nico: "You
won't be invited."

"Disgusting." Nico makes a show of considering his tiles.
"Don't even tell me. I guarantee you, I won't want to know."

"Actually, it's a fascinating biological phenomenon."
Theophrastos looks up from his book. "When we're home,
we'll dissect a pregnant sheep together. It's quite similar."

"Fun!" Nico says.

"Oh, fun." Herpyllis swats at him across the table.
"Disgusting, both of you. Theophrastos, you're as bad as their
father was. Dead animals all over the house, and always some

carcass boiling away in my kitchen so he could preserve the skeleton. Pytho, you look tired."

My cue. "I am, rather. I think I'll say goodnight."

I make the rounds of kissing cheeks and none of them quite looks at me. I wonder who Herpyllis *hasn't* told.

"I thought we'd go out to the farm tomorrow," I say. "Take a picnic."

Everyone agrees that is a first-rate idea.

I wash in the big room and change into my nightdress. By the time I'm done, the courtyard is empty. Herpyllis's doing, no doubt. I cross to Nicanor's room.

"Yes," he calls.

I open the door. The room is dark, but he's not sleeping; I can feel his tense alertness, even flat on his back in the narrow bed.

"We thought to visit the farm tomorrow, for a picnic. We'd—I'd like it if you came."

He breathes out.

"May I come in?" When he doesn't answer, I close the door behind me and place the lamp on the table. "May I sit?"

"Pythias."

I sit on the edge of the bed.

"Pytho."

"Herpyllis says I should ask if you have an injury."

"Ah."

We sit for a moment, breathing in the excellently honest silence.

"No," he says.

I touch the tie at my shoulder.

"No." He pulls my hand down, quickly, and holds it in both of his own. "I don't want you to do that."

I tell myself: he would do it if it meant nothing to him. I tell myself: therefore, it means something. He's packed in thorny burnet, still, or I am. Packed in spikes, both of us, until we arrive at a safe place.

I go back to my room.

The next morning he's there for breakfast, and supervises the packing up of our caravan. He's fast and silent at the work, and when he's done, he and Pyrrhaios go for the horses. "Will you ride?" Nicanor asks me over his shoulder.

"Yes."

We all ride, in the end, even Herpyllis, her arms around Pyrrhaios's waist. Nicanor slings the picnic in saddlebags so we won't have to bother with the cart.

"Army-style," Theophrastos says.

If this is criticism, or snobbery, it's lost on my little brother. He seems taken with his big cousin, my husband, and nips around on his pony, asking questions about army life and army style. For the moment, anyway, Nicanor tolerates him.

As for me, something happened to me last night when he turned me away. Now, when he comes back to us after being somewhere far away inside himself—a word or two in his deep voice; his sudden frail, sweet smile—I catch my breath. When his eyes pass over me, I feel it. I know this is probably only because he is indifferent to me, but there is something in that indifference that I feel in the palms of my hands. My vanity is pricked; I'm humiliated, challenged. Stumped. Where's the way in?

Demetrios is in the yard in front of Euphranor's farm with a couple of slaves, sorting through a cart loaded with bags of seed. The slaves open each bag and call out the contents while Demetrios ticks them off on a tablet. A new delivery; spring is here. Demetrios looks up as we pass, raises a hand in greeting, and returns to his work.

"What do they plant?" Nicanor is beside me for a moment.

"Wheat, barley. A few vegetables—onions, beans. Mostly it's grain, though, for export to Athens. That's where the money is. The trees are oak and chestnut. A few fruit trees."

"Vines?"

"Not on our property." I point with my chin—we're here. "It's run down." *A bit run down*, I was going to say, but that would be wrong. "I couldn't—"

He grunts, rides ahead, dismounts. Looks around. Breathes deep. Looks up at the sky through the treetops, then down at the dirt. Kicks at it with his toe; squats to run some through his fingers. Shades his eyes to look into the abandoned fields, into the sun. He's all here.

I get myself down while Pyrrhaios helps Herpyllis. I suppose I should have waited for my husband, or Theophrastos, who takes my reins with a reproving look. Ladies are unfamiliar with horses, I suppose, even getting themselves off them.

"Thank you," I say to him.

Surprised, he softens. "You ride well."

"My father permitted it."

I see in his face a tiny recalibration: his future wife will be permitted to ride, too. A wedding gift I've thrown blind at some anonymous woman; a gift I've hurled at the future, too, if he decides to write about it and influence other men that way. Perhaps, in the future, women will be taught to ride as part of their educations, all because of my lie just now, my four little words. Fun!

"Pythias."

I actually trip over my feet in my hurry to answer Nicanor's call. I see Herpyllis exchange a fond look with Pyrrhaios. They must think it happened last night.

"Will you show me around?"

I ask Herpyllis if she will supervise setting up the picnic, here in the yard. It's cool, still, even in the sun; too cool and dew-edged for the pond.

"Take your time," she says. "Blanket?" I glare at her, but she's unembarrassed. "It has to be done at some point."

She's right, of course, that and the sacrifices before the first crops go in, but luckily Nicanor is already walking, and didn't hear.

"Next time," I say. "I think right now he just wants me to show him around."

As we walk, I sketch the layout of the farm: fields, orchard, river, pond, woods. I collect specimens as we go: snail shells, flowers for pressing, a yellow and black striped millipede that I carry in my hand. It wriggles. I let it clamber from finger to finger while we walk.

"Insects, eh?" Nicanor says.

"It's for Nico. I prefer birds. Fish, too, but mostly birds. I had to leave my collection in Athens."

"Who cares for them?"

I don't understand, and then I do. He thinks I mean they're alive.

"Skeletons," I say. "I collect skeletons."

"We're behind, if our neighbours already have their seed." His mind has moved on. "I'd like to spend a lot of time here. Maybe even make the house liveable again. For me, at least. The well's still good?"

"Yes."

"I'd like to see the river." We cut through the stalks and stubble until the babble is louder. "Excellent," he says. "No crops without irrigation." He stands, hands on his hips, and looks all around again.

"You've never farmed, have you?" I ask.

He rewards me with his rare smile. "Never."

"Why are you so keen?"

He looks at his feet. "It's quiet out here," he says finally. "I can think clearly."

As we walk back through the trees to the picnic, we pass a bird's nest lying broken in the long grass. Still teasing the millipede from finger to finger, I go look. There are eggs in it still, one broken, and nearby a newly-hatched dead wren, unfletched, with a disproportionately large head and bulging eyes.

Nicanor comes to look, too. "Fell down."

I shake my head. "Starlings, probably. They're looters. Here." Awkwardly, I transfer the millipede from my fingers to his so I can pick up the dead chick. The head lolls. It doesn't fill the palm of my hand.

"What are you going to do with that?"

Back in the yard, Herpyllis has laid the picnic out on

blankets. Nico is delighted by the millipede, and everyone crowds around to see my prize.

"Filthy, disgusting children," Herpyllis says. "And I brought cold chicken for lunch."

After we've eaten, Pyrrhaios, Theophrastos and Nicanor walk over to pick Demetrios's brains. They come back full of purpose, and immediately set about making lists. Herpyllis says she wants a nap, so I offer to show Nico the nest.

"I might have done something bad," Nico says as we walk. "I asked Nicanor to tell me about the siege of Tyre. Theophrastos said I should ask."

"Why is that bad?"

"I'm not sure."

We've reached the nest. Nico squats next to it and fingers through the broken egg shells.

At last he says, "He told me to mind my own business."

Together we pick the shards from the nest. Gingerly, Nico lifts the nest from the grass. It stays together.

"Well, I got kind of mad. I mean, that was just rude for no reason. So I bugged him a little. I mean, I kept asking. It was for Theophrastos, really."

"Theophrastos could have asked for himself." I tear a strip from the hem of my dress to wrap the nest in, so he can carry it suspended by the knot and hopefully get it home in one piece.

"I think Theophrastos is scared of him. You know he stutters, Theophrastos, when he's nervous? He's afraid sometimes he won't get the words out. I know you don't like him much, Pytho, but sometimes I feel sorry for him. He's very nervous, and he knows he'll never be as smart as Daddy."

My brother is no longer a child.

"So you pressed Nicanor. Then what?"

He shakes his head, remembering. Just when I think he isn't going to answer, he says, "He told me he'd seen men die in ways I couldn't imagine, and if I were his son he'd cripple me so I'd never have to serve in the army. I told him I wasn't a coward and he laughed." Nico flushes, remembering. "He said I didn't know what I was, and hopefully I never would. What does that mean?"

"I don't know."

"Herpyllis worries he isn't kind to you."

*Kind to me.* Is that what sex is?

"She worries he won't take good care of you. She says he's like Daddy used to be, always going off by himself to his room. But Daddy worked and Nicanor does nothing. She says he drinks too much."

"So does Pyrrhaios."

"Pyrrhaios is happy, though."

9⊙8

At home, late that night, Herpyllis finds me in the kitchen.

"I just wanted a hug," she says, putting her arms around me from behind while I tend my pot on the stove. "It doesn't seem so long 'til summer, does it, when we'll see you again?"

"Mm," I say, stirring.

"What are you making? Smells like—" She looks over my shoulder and abruptly lets go of me. "Disgusting!" she says.

When the meat has boiled from the bones, I drain the pot

and lay the bits out on a rag to cool. The skeleton has come completely apart; some of the bones are no bigger than my fingernail clippings. I'll have a puzzle in the morning.

I go to Nicanor's room. "Tell me about Tyre," I say.

He shakes his head without opening his eyes. "Go to bed, Pythias."

"Tell me about India."

He opens his eyes.

"Tell me about Persia. Tell me about Babylon. Tell me about Kandahar. Talk to me."

Harshly now: "Go to bed."

I remove the pins at my shoulders and the front of my dress falls to my lap.

"No." He actually writhes, rolling his head one way and then the other, trying not to see. "No."

"Do you want a boy?"

"No."

"Is it because of how I spent my time while you were away?"

He sits up and covers one of my meagre breasts with his palm. The nipple hardens. He's actually considering laying me. Conversation is worse?

"No." He takes his hand from my breast and touches my chin, lifts it slightly in an echo of the widow's gesture, until I have to look at his face. "Not tonight. Tomorrow."

"Really?"

He lifts my dress back to my shoulders.

۹۰۸

The next morning, I lay the bones out on a cloth in the courtyard, for the good, early light. I start easy: the skull; the vertebrae, which are tiny but distinctive; the humeri and scapulae—shoulders and arms in people, wings in the bird. Daddy taught me that.

Nico wanders into the courtyard with his bread and honey, to watch and offer an occasional suggestion. Herpyllis next, with her tea. She's enjoying the two of us together, rather than our reconstruction. Pyrrhaios appears to tell us he's loaded the carts, and Pinch is ready for Nico. We bid goodbye in front of the house. No tears this time; we are a sticky spider-web now, connected from Athens to Chalcis and Stageira, and know we cannot be unclipped from each other. We will meet again in a few weeks' time, for Theophrastos's wedding, in Athens.

Nicanor and Theophrastos appear for the final parting; they've been in some deep conversation, and embrace briefly before Theophrastos turns to me to thank me, over-formally, for our hospitality.

"Advising him on the married life?" I ask my husband without looking at him, my hand still raised, suspending the thread between my palm and Herpyllis's, as she looks back from the cart that's just disappearing round the corner at the end of our street. Nicanor sniffs hard and quirks his mouth, holding onto a surprised laugh.

"I'm funny, just so you know," I say.

I turn back to the courtyard, and my chick. At first I think he hasn't followed me, and reconcile myself to a morning alone with my project. But then he's back with a tray, and I see he's detoured through the kitchen to bring bread and tea. "I want to go back to the farm today," he says. "As soon as you're ready."

I don't answer immediately. I'm trying to fit the humerus and scapula together, those tiny bone flutes. Most of the very smallest bones I can't begin to identify. I've laid the big ones together on the cloth: skull, pubis, keel. You can see the baby's shape.

"How will you fix it together?"

I feel his breath on my ear, smell him: leather, sweat, the body, and something sweet.

"My father used fish glue."

"Ah."

He watches for another minute, then leaves again. When he comes back, he's got my travelling cloak over his arm.

"I'm busy," I say.

He sits down to wait.

I work for a few more minutes, then turn to the tray.

"Why do you suppose no one's ever seen a centaur?" Nicanor asks.

"Centaurs live in Thrace."

"I've been to Thrace," Nicanor says.

I sip my tea.

"What I *have* seen," Nicanor says, "are monkeys. In India. Do you know what a monkey is?"

"No."

"They're like little people, with hair all over them and long tails and overlong arms and legs. They chatter like they're speaking a language."

I take a bit of bread, but Nicanor puts his hand over mine to stop me.

"Pytho, listen," he says. "I've killed so many people, I lost count. I tried to keep count but I got confused. And when you torch a village, it's hard to tally. How many died, exactly? How many I was responsible for myself, and how many I would have

to share?"

Figs, too.

"I saw the king. Many times. I always thought of your father. It was hard to imagine them in a room together. Alexander was so—"

I wait.

"He had the strangest eyes," he said. "When he wasn't fighting, he looked confused. Does that make any sense? And tired. He was always so tired. He seemed so old and tired and broken, but in your father's stories he was this burning boy."

"Daddy wrote him letters. He never wrote back, but he collected specimens and sent them by courier."

Nicanor shrugs. "I wouldn't know about that."

"He says he wrote the king about you. Alerting him to your presence, and stressing your relationship. Suggesting he might—make use of your talents, or your intelligence, somehow. Befriend you."

Nicanor raises his eyebrows.

"Daddy taught him to swim."

Nicanor rubs his forehead, then says, "He couldn't swim. We saw him try, in India. He wanted us to swim across the river at Nysa, to surprise the enemy from behind. He waded in and flailed around and wouldn't let anyone touch him. He looked like a cat in a rain barrel. He even tried to float across on his own shield. When he couldn't do it, he made us march to a shallower place where we could ford it. Gods, that was a long day."

"And did you surprise the enemy from behind?"

He makes a tired gesture that means yes. "Are you ready?"

I let him help me with my cloak, but I mount by myself. Tycho follows us on a donkey. I say, "I didn't know we had a donkey."

"I bought him yesterday."

"What's his name?"

Nicanor has to think about that. "Snit," he says finally.

"What?"

"Snit."

I look at him.

"I'm funny, too," he says.

We turn the corner where we'd waved Herpyllis and the others out of sight. There's the town spread out below us, the near side and the far, and the tender green farmland beyond. The sun shaves sparks off the blue water. We can see movement in the town, all the tiny people making things work, and even the ferryman with his barge and his pole, tiny, tiny.

"Snitty," I say, and he agrees that's even better.

"What *did* Daddy teach him, do you suppose?" I ask. "I mean, that stuck."

He thinks for a moment, then says we should get going.

࿓

At the farm, he tells me to wait at the edge of a muddy field. When he wades out into the middle of it with a blanket, he disappears to the ankles. Tycho and I watch him lay the blanket flat and tromp back.

"Tycho will hold your sandals," Nicanor says.

He takes my hand and leads me through the sucking mud to the blanket, while Tycho waits with his back to us at the edge of the field with our horses and Snitty and my sandals and the picnic. I lie down on my back. My husband lowers himself onto me, eyes closed. It takes a while, but finally his seed comes. He lets his full weight rest on me while his breathing recovers. When he gets off me, I reach down and wipe some of the seed onto my fingers. It's like mucus. I fling what I can into the field, and he offers me the hem of his clothes to wipe the rest on. I think of the women drugged by the god. This is nothing like that. This is bright sun, cold, mud, and my husband unsmiling. This is outdoors, daytime, bright pain, and cold. He pats my shoulder and walks away.

We return to Tycho, who's laid out the picnic. I take my sandals and a towel and tell them I'm going to the river to wash off. When I come back, they're sitting together, eating, talking. When Tycho sees me, he starts to get up, but I tell him, "Stay."

Our lunch is bread and cheese. Nicanor has rigged up a bar over a cook fire so he can hang a pot from it to heat something for us to sip. Hot water. They're talking about crops.

"My father belonged to a farmer," Tycho says. "I lived with him until my beard came in. I can tell you what I know."

*Teach*, he can't bring himself to say.

"I would be grateful," Nicanor says.

"I didn't know that about you," I say to Tycho.

"Lady," he says, ducking his head in acknowledgement. He hesitates, then says to Nicanor, "It's good here."

Nicanor looks up at him.

"Good air, good water, good soil." He's holding Nicanor's gaze, unusually. "Quiet."

"It *is* quiet," Nicanor says.

"A good place to come," Tycho says.

Nicanor nods.

Tycho leaves us then, ostensibly to look at what needs doing first to the farmhouse.

"A bit forward, that one," Nicanor says.

"Daddy was the one who bought him when his beard came in," I say. "For heavy work. I've known him all my life. He's loyal, but he does always find a way of saying what's on his mind."

"He wants me to farm," Nicanor says.

"Apparently."

We pack up the lunch things, and Nicanor kicks dirt over the fire.

"Well." I flutter my fingers toward the fields. "Same time next year?"

I win another smile. He slings an arm across my shoulders and squeezes, briefly. "Sure," he whispers into my hair.

❧

Back at home, there's a commotion in front of our house. An enormous cart is tethered out front, and Olympios is supervising the unloading of a massive marble sculpture. "The other one's already inside," he says, when we come close.

They lean the two pieces up side by side in the courtyard. "Do you know about this?" Nicanor asks, while the driver waits, narrow-eyed, for his pay.

I'm blank, and it's Tycho who answers. I remember as he's saying it: Daddy sent Simon to Athens to commission statues to Zeus and Athena to commemorate Nicanor's safe return. They're to be erected in Stageira, but the cost of transport being what it was, Daddy only wanted to pay to have them sent as far as Chalcis; we'd have to take them the rest of the way ourselves. They'll watch us from now on: Zeus, big-chested and big-bearded, with the piercing eyes; Athena of the clear brow and crested helmet. Here they will remain for many months, eerie at first and later familiar, finally just furniture.

Nicanor pays the driver and says he's going to his room. He asks Tycho to send his tray there. I feel the ghostly throb of him still in my vagina, but realize we have had no easy breakthrough, and there will be no cosy cuddling in the marital bed tonight. We have done what we can to ensure agricultural good luck, and who knows what soup is cooking inside me now, but in his mind my husband is still in Egypt, Persia, Bactria, Kandahar, India, Babylon—torching villages, raping peasant girls, starving, night-marching, eternally suffering under the obsession of an eternally suffering king. Wren bones and fish glue, indeed.

I could end it here. But there is one more thing to mention: a gift I asked of my husband, a wedding gift. At first he was reluctant.

"Oh, pink cloth," I said. "Poof. Pink cloth. What am I supposed to do with that, sew myself a dress?" The chick was done by then, as done as he was going to be, and hanging from the ceiling in the big bedroom by a piece of thread. He flew in the slightest breeze. I don't see what's gruesome.

"Fine," my husband said. "But don't come crying to me when you have regrets." We weren't sharing the room—probably never would—but we used it for private conversations, particularly concerning the servants. It was high spring by then, and he was mostly living at the farm, camping out there with the men he employed. He came home every now and then for a bath and a meal, and some evenings when he'd seemed less distant than usual I'd visit him in his room, then return to my own for sleep. He'd got the good Euboia dirt grained into his hands by then, under the nails, and maybe he drank a little less. I never asked him, nor Thale neither, who kept the stores and would know.

"You'll have to come with us, to the magistrate."

"Have you considered terms?"

"As few as possible," I said. "It's what my father would have wanted."

So today we return to the home of Plios the magistrate. My husband is resentful that I've kept him from the fields; he was late getting the seed in, and his inexperience makes him anxious. But then he is proud, too, shyly proud of the pale green nubs he's already coaxed from the mud. I've begun a vegetable patch by the house so we'll have something to talk about in the evenings. The first harvest from that patch, an early lettuce, I've brought as a gift for the magistrate's wife. Tycho follows us at his usual distance, leading Frost. Nicanor plans to ride straight from the magistrate back to the farm.

"I've been thinking I might do some teaching," I say as we walk. "Girls from wealthy families. Do you remember Thaulos? He asked if I'd teach his daughter to read. Maybe a bit of math, a bit of biology. There's a fashion for it." I finger the stone and the snail-shell from Daddy's school that I've taken to carrying in my pocket, lately, as talismans. I've already started with Pretty; she can say her alphabet very nicely, and she likes it when I draw numbers on her tickly back with my finger and she has to guess what they are. Slow Philo likes to watch us, squatting on his heels, clapping his hands when Pretty laughs. Once he held up three fingers to show her and said in his thick voice, "Three."

Pretty looked at me. I told her she had two teachers now. Philo beamed.

"Not for money," Nicanor says now.

"Of course not."

"I wouldn't set them on skeletons, either," he says. "Not right away, anyway."

"I've been meaning to ask you to bring me a fox, if you find one. I've never done a fox. I know farmers kill them if they can."

"Chicken farmers," Nicanor says dismissively. Then: "I'll see what I can do. I'll ask Demetrios. He has traps."

He's made friends with Demetrios, and Euphranor too, who is beyond deferential. Star-struck, almost, by my husband's experiences in Alexander's army, by his hard edge and remote silences. Star-struck, lovestruck. He looks a little silly, these days, Euphranor. But he's helping enormously with the farm, and says he'll put my husband in touch with an honest dealer when it comes time to sell the harvest to Athens, in the fall.

"Come, Tycho," Nicanor says. Tycho follows us through Plios's gate. A slave leads us into an inner room, Plios's office, where the magistrate rises from his desk to greet us. I'm heavily veiled; he ignores me.

"This is the fellow?" he asks, and Nicanor says yes.

"A great day for you," Plios says to Tycho.

I pay the token coin to Plios—a privilege I had particularly asked of my husband. I wanted to do it myself. I put the coin on his desk, like a lady, so our hands won't touch.

"You are no longer a slave," Nicanor tells Tycho. "But your obligation to the family will remain until your death. You will come to us three times each month for instruction. These are the formal terms. Additionally, you will owe a freedman's tax to the city. Any children you might have will be exempt from this tax. Plios the magistrate represents the city as our witness."

"Children *I* might have?" Tycho says.

"Done!" Plios says, most jolly. "Now. Do we have time for a cup?"

A slave brings a tray with a jug and three cups for the men. Tycho looks like he's going to throw up.

"Drink, man!" Plios says. "Look at him. He's terrified. Where are the others, anyway? I thought we were doing four today."

Of course, as magistrate, he's read Daddy's will: *And Tycho, Philo, Olympios, and his child shall have their freedom when my daughter is married.*

"Their terms are different," Nicanor says. "No rush there."

Outside, Nicanor mounts Frost. My hand has strayed to my belly again; I see him look, look away. "Walk her home, will you?" my husband says to Tycho. "I'll be a week at least. Your lady will explain everything to you. So." He spurs the horse and is gone, my unmoved mover: gone without a backward look.

He'll probably remember my fox, though.

"Lady," Tycho says. "I don't have money for the tax."

We walk; not home, but to the beach where my father swam and then washed up, where Euphranor saw my birthmark, where Myrmex and I fucked each other all ways. We sit on the flat rock where Daddy used to leave his clothes. "You can have the shed behind the stables," I tell Tycho. The biggest of the outbuildings. "I've been fixing it up. It's clean and dry, weather-tight. I put in a new bedroll, and a chair and a lamp, and a chest for your things. You'll keep working for us, only we'll pay you now. And you'll have free time, to do what you want."

We sit for a long time, quietly, as morning turns hot noon.

"Children," he says.

I put my head on his shoulder, and after a while he puts his arm around me.

## ACKNOWLEDGEMENTS

Huge thanks to Professor Susan Downie and Professor Shane Hawkins, of Carleton University; Professor Pauline Ripat and Professor Mark Golden, of the University of Winnipeg; and Professor Maria Liston, of the University of Waterloo, for sharing their vast knowledge.

Thanks to Anna Avdeeva for her generous gift of *Medicinal Plants of Greece* and Conni Bagnall for Robert Graves's *The Greek Myths*.

Thanks to Anna Avdeeva, Amanda Holmes, Ariel Levine and Christine Lorimer of Carleton University and the University of Winnipeg, who came to Aristotle's Lyceum with me.

The poem Pythias reads on the road to Chalcis is from *If Not, Winter: Fragments of Sappho*, translated by Anne Carson.

The iunx spell Pythias recites is a combination of four incantations cited by Christopher A. Faraone in *Ancient Greek Love Magic*.

Thanks as always to Anne Collins and Denise Bukowski, my colleagues and friends.

ANNABEL LYON's first novel, *The Golden Mean*, was the winner of the Rogers Writers' Trust Fiction Prize and a finalist for the Scotiabank Giller Prize, the Governor General's Literary Award, the Ethel Wilson Fiction Prize, and the Commonwealth Writers' Prize. *The Golden Mean* became a #1 bestseller in Canada and has been translated into fourteen languages. Among Lyon's other works are *Oxygen*, a short-story collection nominated for the Danuta Gleed Award, and *The Best Thing for You*, a collection of novellas that was nominated for the Ethel Wilson Fiction Prize. Before Lyon decided to write full-time, she studied classical music, philosophy, and law and taught piano. She lives in Vancouver with her partner and two children.

A NOTE ABOUT THE TYPE

*The Sweet Girl* has been set in Centaur, designed originally for New York's Metropolitan Museum in 1914, then adapted for general use in 1929. While a so-called modern face, Centaur is modelled on letters cut by the fifteenth-century printer Nicolas Jenson. Its italic, originally named Arrighi, was designed in 1925 and is based on the work of Ludovico degli Arrighi, a Renaissance scribe. Centaur is considered among the finest, most elegant faces for book-length work.